Make Me Yours

M. S Parker

ISBN-13: 978-1535459976
ISBN-10: 1535459972

Table of Contents

Chapter 1

Hanna

I heard him moving around the room but kept my eyes down, my hands clasped behind my back. The cool air caressed my bare skin, making my nipples tighten even harder than they already were. I'd been kneeling like this for only a few minutes, but in the playroom, time seemed to stretch and bend in all sorts of ways. There weren't any clocks in here because when it was time to play, Cross always made sure we didn't have anything else planned for the remainder of the day.

He liked to take his time.

It was hard to believe that we'd been together for nearly five months. I'd come to Hollywood to get some distance from my parents and to spend time with my older sister, Juliette, but I hadn't planned on staying. Not exactly, anyway. All I'd known was that I hadn't wanted to go back to Zanesville, Ohio to spend the rest of my life managing the family business and taking a backseat to my perfect brother, RJ.

Then I'd met Cross Phillips, the thirty-year-old billionaire who'd introduced me to the BDSM lifestyle and stolen my heart. I'd been attracted to him from the first time I met him, and his presence during my sister's abduction had only solidified my feelings for him. Four months ago, after my sister had been found safe and the people responsible were in jail, Cross had given me a collar.

Though I was still new to the lifestyle, I understood the level of commitment that came when a Dom gave a Sub a collar. It was a mark of ownership. Not like some freaky sex slave thing where he controlled every aspect of my life, but rather a way of letting others in that world know that I was taken.

That collar, a delicate silver choker designed to look enough like a necklace that I could wear it in public, was the only thing I had on at the moment. I wore it as often as I could, even if it didn't always look right with what I was wearing. He hadn't asked me to keep it on all the time, but I loved watching his slate gray eyes light up when he saw me with it on, especially when he hadn't asked for it.

Today, however, he'd sent me a bouquet of irises – my favorite flower – with a card that had given me clear instructions. Well, clear to me anyway.

Put on my favorite outfit as soon as you get to my place. I have a special evening planned.

I'd spent the rest of the day at work completely distracted, my pussy throbbing in anticipation. I knew all too well the sorts of decadent things that awaited me in Cross's playroom.

Even though I still technically lived with my sister, I spent enough time at his house to have space for my own clothes. I also had my own key. I used it to let myself in after work, then I'd done as he'd asked.

His favorite "outfit" was my collar. Nothing more.

So when he'd arrived home, I'd been waiting in the

2

middle of the living room, wearing only the thin chain.

There were times when Cross wanted me hard and fast, but tonight would be one of those times he dragged things out. We'd eaten dinner with him only removing his jacket, tie, and shoes. I was completely naked. When we'd finished, we cleaned up, and only then had he touched me. Barely a brush of his lips against mine, but it was my signal – we were about to begin.

That had been ten minutes ago, and I was starting to get impatient. Cross could be demanding at times, but when he decided he wanted to take things slow, nothing could change his mind. I'd tried in the past and had ended up getting spanked hard enough to make sitting at work the next day decidedly uncomfortable.

So I waited, listening to him moving around the room, getting things ready for whatever it was he had planned. I couldn't see him, but I could picture him clearly. His tall, muscular frame. Unruly white-blond hair. A classically handsome face that was a touch too rugged to be pretty. And a dimple that made me go weak in the knees when he smiled. Hell, just looking at him was enough to make my legs lose their strength.

I felt him before his feet entered my line of sight. When I saw his bare legs, I knew he'd stripped, and my stomach clenched. As gorgeous as he looked in everything he wore, his nude form was the sort of thing artists would fight over. I desperately wanted to look up, to let my gaze travel up his muscular legs to that narrow waist and all the deliciousness in between, but I knew I had to wait for his permission.

"Look at me."

I almost sighed in relief. For me, the anticipation was always the worst part. Well, that, and when he wouldn't let me touch him. I hated that.

3

When I raised my eyes, I took my time, savoring every inch of tanned skin, toned muscle. By the time I reached his face, my pulse had quickened, my breathing increased. When my gaze met his, I almost forgot to breathe.

"Open." The command was ragged, telling me that this wouldn't be some gentle sensation play or a bit of bondage. Cross wanted more, and I wanted whatever he would give me.

I opened my mouth, clenching my hands as I fought the urge to touch him. When the head of his cock slipped between my parted lips, I shivered. He ran his fingers through my wild curls, fisting them as his heavy shaft slid across my tongue. My hair had grown a bit since we'd first been together, mostly because he liked holding it, pulling it. I liked it too.

"Put a hand on my hip," he ordered.

I obeyed, keeping my other hand behind my back. I knew what was coming, but he said it anyway. That's how we did things. He'd tell me what he planned to do, giving me the chance to use my safe word. I hadn't used it yet, probably because he always prepared me, but he loved taking me to the edge of my comfort zone, and then giving the smallest of nudges.

I also loved listening to his voice describing all of the things he wanted to do, he was going to do.

"Two taps on my hip if you can't say your safe word," he instructed. "Nod if you understand."

It wasn't easy to nod with a mouthful of cock, but I managed. My tongue twitched against him, eager to explore.

"I'm going to fuck your mouth." It sounded almost conversational, the way he said it. "Create some suction, but don't do anything else."

4

I nodded again to show that I understood. Then his hand tightened in my hair, and he began to move. He started slow, gauging how far I could take him. I took slow breaths through my nose, then felt the urge to gag as the tip of him reached the back of my throat. My fingers curled into his hip, and he paused. When I didn't tap out, he kept going, holding my head in place as I automatically struggled against him as he went deeper.

"Relax, baby," he murmured. "You can do it, I know you can."

Some part of my mind still wanted to argue when he said things like that, but I knew he had a sixth sense for this sort of thing, for knowing what I could handle, for just how much he could test my limits. So I let him fill me completely, let him hold me there for several seconds before pulling out. I coughed and gasped, feeling a burning in my throat, but when his cock brushed my lips again, I didn't even hesitate.

This time, he wasn't so easy, but he also didn't go as far. Instead, he held my head tight and rocked his hips, thrusting in my mouth with shallow, brisk strokes. I had no control, could do nothing but suck on him as he fucked my mouth, but I never once considered ending it. I trusted him. He was in control, but I had the power, and that dynamic was what made us work.

Without warning, he pulled out and took a step back. "Up."

I stood, panting hard as I tried to calm my breathing. He handed me a towel to wipe my face and then gestured toward the bed.

"Bend over, hands on the bed, feet shoulder width apart."

I obeyed, the cool air brushing the wet skin between my legs.

5

"I told you once that a skilled Dom could make a Sub come with a flogger."

I closed my eyes. Shit. He had talked about it, but I'd never really paid much attention since the conversations usually took place during moments like these. The entire time we'd been together, he'd stuck to using his hand when he spanked me.

"Now I'll show you how it's done."

I heard the sound of a drawer opening, closing, then a gentle swishing. I jumped when the strips of leather touched me, even though he was only running them up and down my spine, my ass. I gasped as he moved them up between my legs, rubbing against me until I was moaning deep in my chest.

Then it was gone. I barely had time to process it before he brought the flogger down again, with force this time. It didn't hurt, exactly, not even as much as his hand did, but a warm, tingling feeling spread across my skin. Three more strikes came down in quick succession, alternating cheeks.

I yelped as the fourth blow came up between my legs. It wasn't hard at all, but the sensation was different from anything I'd felt before. The next one made me shudder. The next stung. He switched to my ass, then back to my pussy. Back and forth, he increased the intensity of the strikes until each one had a bite of pain with the pleasure.

"Spread your lips."

I bit my bottom lip to hold in a whimper, but I moved one hand beneath me and used my fingers to hold myself open. My skin was hot under my fingers, more sensitive to my touch than it had ever been.

I closed my eyes and braced myself for what I knew was coming next.

The jolt of pain was immediately followed by a burst of white-hot pleasure. When the second one landed, I came. My head fell forward, my body tensing, shuddering through the bliss. A strong arm wrapped around my waist, holding me up for a moment before turning me over and sliding me back onto the bed. I whimpered as my ass rubbed against the expensive sheets. I was on fire.

Cross held my legs apart as he followed me onto the bed. My back arched, a cry coming from my lips as he ran his tongue over the sensitive, burning flesh between my legs. He tossed my thighs over his shoulders and began to use his mouth to soothe me. I writhed against him, dug my fingers into the sheets to keep from touching his head, from holding him against me while he drove me to a second, then third orgasm.

I was still shaking when he flipped me over. His hands, slick with a cool lotion, moved over my ass, easing the sting and burn. When he spread my cheeks, I waited for a probing finger, but what I felt teasing my hole was something else.

His tongue.

He'd talked to me about wanting to do this, but up until now, it'd only been talk. My eyelids fluttered as he worked his tongue over the rim of muscle, then past it. I moaned as a finger joined in, sliding in and out with a slow, steady rhythm. His free hand moved under me, pulling me up so that my ass was in the air and my head stayed on the sheets. After three orgasms, my muscles protested even the slightest effort, but I managed to hold myself up as he added a second finger.

"Where do you want me?" Cross asked as he ran his hand up my stomach to cup one of my breasts. He rolled my nipple between his thumb and forefinger, then gave it a sharp tug. "Do you want my cock in your ass or in your cunt?"

My brain could barely make sense of the words, much less give an answer. At this point, I didn't care. I just wanted to feel him inside me.

"Let me be more specific," he said as he shoved a third finger into me. "One hole gets my cock. The other will be filled with a new toy. I'm giving you the choice of what you want where, but if you don't answer, I'll place a plug in your ass, a vibrator in your cunt, and they'll stay there all night while you suck me off every time I get hard." He leaned over me, three fingers in my ass and his cock hard against my thigh. "So what's it going to be? Where do you want my cock?"

For one terrifying moment, I thought I wouldn't be able to answer, and I'd spend the rest of the night begging for relief. I finally managed to blurt out the first word that popped into my head. "Ass."

"Good girl." He pulled his fingers out, and a shudder ran through me at the sudden loss. "Let's get that new toy ready. And no peeking."

Less than a minute later, cool, hard silicone slid along my slit, teasing my entrance before the head breached me, spreading me wide. A strangled sort of sound came out of me as Cross worked the toy inside. It wasn't smooth like the other toys he'd used. This one had bumps and ridges that rubbed and pressed against my walls as he pushed it into me. And it was big. Easily as big as Cross, and that was saying something. My legs shook as it filled me, one of the bumps pressing against my g-spot as it settled into place.

"How does that feel?" He ran his hand over my back.

All I could manage was a moan. He chuckled, that low, sensual sound that I loved so much.

"I'm going to fuck your ass," he said matter-of-factly

as he ran his hands over my hips. "Come as many times as you want, babe, but make sure you scream my name every time."

Some people might've thought that was a joke, but I'd learned that if he said to scream his name, he meant it. If he felt me come and I didn't do what he said, I'd be punished later.

When he slowly pushed his way inside me, I didn't scream his name, but I did scream, pressing my face to the pillow to muffle the sound. He'd used his fingers and a thin butt plug at the same time as his cock before, but I'd never had two things that size inside me at the same time. I felt like I was being ripped apart, but it wasn't all pain. His movement made the toy inside me shift and rub against my g-spot, coaxing pleasure into my tortured nerves.

He stopped for a moment once he was completely inside, but I knew it was for his own benefit rather than mine. He wanted me to come, wanted to bring me pleasure, but he wanted it done his way. And tonight, that meant rough.

As he began to move, each stroke moving the other shaft as well, I had a moment to remember that there'd been a time when I hadn't realized that I liked things rough, kinky, but now, I couldn't imagine my sex life without it.

Then Cross was pounding into me hard enough to drive the air from my lungs, and I didn't think about anything but the way he made me feel. The pressure inside me was building fast, and before I knew it, I was coming again. I didn't have enough breath to scream, but I managed to get his name out.

"That's my girl," he said as he pinched my nipple.

I made a squeaking sound that made him laugh, and

the vibrations went right through me, pushing me toward yet another climax. This one would be the end of me, I knew. I could barely move, barely breathe. I wondered if I passed out this time, if he'd excuse me for not being able to say a word.

He twisted my nipple hard enough to make my body jerk, jostling the shaft in my pussy. Then his fingers were on my swollen clit, the pressure and friction almost painful, and I came again. I managed a scream this time, repeating his name over and over as his fingers moved relentlessly over my clit, each pass in time with a thrust into my ass. I was still coming when I felt him jerk against me, felt the hot liquid of his cum, his cock pulsing as it emptied.

He curled around me as we both slumped down on the bed. For the moment, neither of us was willing, or able, to move, but I didn't mind. His arms were around me and that was all that mattered.

Chapter 2

Hanna

To say that I was sore from the prior night's activities would have been a massive understatement. Most of my body felt like I'd been involved in some sort of marathon. My pussy and ass both ached in that deep, throbbing way that only came with having had a good, hard fuck. I didn't regret any of it for a second, but it would definitely be distracting at work today.

The way my sister's light violet eyes were dancing as I walked into the apartment said that she knew not only how I felt, but what it had taken to get me there. It wasn't surprising considering Juliette was a much-sought-after Dominatrix, and she'd been doing it long enough to recognize how thoroughly I'd been fucked last night...and again in the shower this morning.

Though we were five years apart, Juliette and I almost looked like twins. We had the same eyes, nearly the same shade of black hair. We were both tall and curvy – though she had a few inches on me in height – and we both had our mother's fine features. When Juliette left Ohio eight years ago, I'd still been in that awkward stage of puberty, but by the time I'd come to California this past summer, the resemblance was enough that people often mistook me for her.

In fact, Cross had done just that. When he'd first approached me, he thought I was Juliette and wanted to know if I'd consider Subbing for him. That's how I'd discovered the lifestyle my sister was a part of. The mistaken identity had made things a bit awkward at first, but he'd quickly made it clear that once he knew who I was, my sister had never crossed his mind again.

"Damn," Juliette said with a grin. "I hope you have enough time to recover before you see Mom and Dad because if you show up looking like that, with Cross on your arm, Dad will have his head...or other body parts I'm sure you're equally fond of."

"Thanks." I let the sarcasm drip from the words. "That's exactly what I needed to hear to make myself less anxious about taking Cross home for Thanksgiving."

"You don't have to go, you know," Juliette said as she poured us both glasses of juice. "We could spend Thanksgiving together."

"Or you could come too," I suggested as I slid into the seat across from her. I picked up one of the cheese wedges she'd set out. "You haven't been home in years."

"This is home," Juliette said firmly. "Not Zanesville. That hasn't been home for me in a long time."

"Mom and Dad would love to see you," I said, hoping guilt would turn her to my side.

She gave me a skeptical look. "Come on, Hanna, we both know better than that. Mom and Dad love me, I know, but they've never forgiven me for leaving."

"Maybe with me moving out here too, they're realizing that it doesn't mean we don't love them," I suggested.

"Or maybe they'll be more upset with me because I corrupted you," she countered.

12

The sad thing was, she had a point. That did sound like the more likely response from our parents. The only one in the family who could never do any wrong was our brother, RJ. His favoritism had been clear enough growing up, and it had only gotten worse when he'd stayed in the area to go to trade school, then gone right into full-time employment in the family auto mechanics business. He'd married his high school sweetheart and even bought the house next door to where we'd grown up. It'd been hard on Juliette growing up with perfect Raymond Jr as a little brother, but being three years younger than him was even worse because I was always in his shadow. No matter how well I did in school, or what accomplishments I achieved, nothing was ever as good as what RJ did.

Then I'd done the unthinkable and joined Juliette on the West Coast. Our parents weren't some backward hicks who thought California was hedonism incarnate, but they did think that family should always come first, which to them meant staying in Ohio and working at the shop under Dad and RJ.

"You'll have to tell me how they react to Cross," Juliette said as she pulled her ebony hair back from her face.

"Yeah, it should be interesting," I said and looked down at my glass. Lunch at home on a Saturday meant I could've had a glass of wine and not felt guilty, but I'd drink what Juliette gave me. I could probably use the extra vitamins anyway.

"What's wrong?" She reached across the table and put her hand on my arm. "You guys didn't have a fight or anything, did you? I mean, you look like you enjoyed yourself last night."

My face warmed. "I did. And I love him..." I let the

13

sentence trail off.

"But?" she prompted.

"Nothing." I shook my head.

"Hanna."

She sounded like our mother when she said my name that way. Not that I'd ever tell her that.

"He never really talks about the future. I mean a week or two, maybe a month if there's something that needs long-term planning, but he never makes any comments that make me believe he's thinking about us long term." I ran my hand through my hair. "Not even something off the cuff, like saying something about a trip in the spring or what he might want to do over some holiday in the future."

"You're worried he doesn't want a traditional relationship." She summed it up quite neatly.

I nodded and took another sip of my drink. "I mean, I have no problem with the sex stuff." My face blazed with heat. "I like it. And we've both said 'I love you,' so I know he's not hung up on that."

"But you want more."

I sighed. "I just want to know that there's a possibility of more. There doesn't have to be a timetable, and it's not like I'm asking to move in with him tomorrow, but I want to know that he sees a future for us."

My sister's face was uncharacteristically somber. "Then you need to talk to him, Hanna. One of the things that both Cross and I told you about the Dom / Sub relationship is true in any relationship. Communication. You have to tell him how you feel."

"I just don't want him to think I'm coming on too strong, that I'm trying to get him to move fast."

The side of Juliette's mouth twitched up in a partial

smile. "Hanna, sweetie, the two of you went from nothing to lovers in a matter of days. I think the ship for 'too fast' has already sailed."

She had a point. Granted, the circumstances surrounding those first few days had been unique, but we hadn't backtracked.

"What if he doesn't want any of that?" My heart thudded painfully even as I asked the question.

"Isn't it better to know now?" she asked softly. "Just talk to him. I've seen the way he looks at you. I'm sure he's just assuming you two will be together, and that he didn't have to bother making any sort of statement. He is a man, after all, and we both know they don't always communicate well when it comes to things like that."

I nodded and told myself that she was right. I needed to talk to Cross, and it would probably all just be some big misunderstanding. I'd feel silly, but we'd keep moving on with our relationship and everything would happen at the right time.

"You know," I said, giving her my best little sister look. "It would make things a lot easier if Cross wasn't alone in the family crossfire all week."

Juliette's eyes narrowed.

"Come on, Jul. You don't have to go early like me and Cross, but you could fly in Wednesday night, then back out on Friday or on the weekend. If we're both there, we can share all the shit Mom and Dad dish out."

She glared at me, then stabbed viciously at a piece of cheese. "You can be such a brat sometimes."

I grinned at her. "But you love me and you know it."

She sighed. "I do, and I suppose that means I'm going home for Thanksgiving."

I squealed and threw myself across the table to hug her. While not completely gone, knowing that Juliette would be there eased a lot of the anxiety in me. Now, if I just got things settled with Cross, everything would be perfect.

Chapter 3

Cross

I was born into a family who still believed in the hard-working ideals that our immigrant ancestors had brought over with them when they'd first come to this country. My father had started showing me the ropes of the family business as soon as I was able to understand the concepts. I'd worked internships in all the various branches from the time I was twelve, and I was only paid what a regular employee at the same level would get. I knew what it was like to have to prove myself to people who only thought of me as a spoiled rich kid. When I was twenty-two, my parents were both killed in a plane crash and I had to take over the rest of the family business even though the board believed I was too young.

I knew what it was like to have to prove myself to people over and over again, knew what it was like to have people judge me by how I looked, who they thought I was. And I never cared about any of it. I knew who I was, knew that I'd worked my ass off to be where I was. That nothing had been handed to me. I'd earned everything. I wasn't worried about being liked or impressing anyone.

Until now.

Hanna and I were on my private jet, heading to Zanesville for Thanksgiving, and I'd never been more nervous in my life. I'd spoken in front of billionaire CEOs, negotiated deals with world-class assholes, and done business in some unsavory places. I'd bluffed my way in contract negotiations and dined with world leaders. All of it had been thrilling, just another form of an adrenaline rush. But the thought of meeting Hanna's family scared the shit out of me.

I'd never met the parents of any woman I'd ever been with. Well, except my high school girlfriend, but I'd technically known her parents before we'd gone on our first date. I hadn't done the whole holiday family thing with them though. Every woman after that, however, had been merely sexual partners. The only exception to that rule – until Hanna – had been the woman who'd introduced me to the BDSM world, but while she'd been more than a simple partner, she was a loner like me. No outside attachments. No "coming home to meet the folks."

I wasn't even sure I knew how to act around a family anymore. It'd been eight years since my parents died, and my social skills in those sorts of situations were rusty. I'd met Juliette, of course, and had spent plenty of time with her in the past few months, but that was different. She was like me, so I understood how to talk to her. We knew a lot of the same people, both in the BDSM world and in Hollywood society.

Raymond and Caroline Breckenridge, however, were unknown entities. They were business people, but their family business and mine were completely different. Their lives were different. I didn't think I was better than them, or above them. I just had no idea how to interact with them.

"Cross."

Judging by how Hanna was saying my name, she'd said it more than once. I forced a smile as I turned to look at her. "Sorry, babe, I was just thinking."

She raised an eyebrow and put her hand on my arm. "You look like you're about to go to your execution. I know Ohio isn't exactly California, but it's not like it's the ninth circle of hell."

That managed to get a partial smile out of me, but at least it was a real one this time. "Only the third, right?"

She laughed, and the sound went right through me. After my first girlfriend and I broke up, I'd only been with experienced women, ones who knew what they wanted and how they wanted it. Hanna, however, was a rare combination of innocence and an insatiable sexual appetite. When she smiled or laughed, her face lit up, and she didn't try to hide it.

"Look, I know Juliette and I don't always talk about our parents in the most glowing of terms, but they're good people." Hanna reached up and ran her fingers through my hair.

My cock gave an interested twitch. Damn, I loved it when she did that.

"There's the usual difficulties that come with kids following their own path, but they've always wanted what's best for us."

Now I wasn't sure who she was trying to convince, me or herself.

"They'll love you," she said firmly. "I'm sure of it."

She leaned over and kissed my cheek. My stomach clenched, and I knew what I needed to relax, to get my head back together. I grasped her chin and ran my thumb along her bottom lip. Her irises darkened to an even deeper shade of violet as I pressed my thumb into her mouth.

Arousal spiked in me as she sucked on my thumb, scraped the pad with her teeth. I gave her a hard look, and she nodded, acknowledging that she understood what I wanted. What I needed.

"On your knees." My voice was hoarse. I was suddenly glad that I only had one steward on the plane and that he stayed in the cockpit with the captain unless I called for him.

She slid to the floor in front of me. Her hands rested on my knees, moving them apart as she settled between them. She knew where this would end up, but she still waited for me to give her instructions.

"Unbutton your shirt."

She was wearing a nice but not overly dressy blouse, and underneath, her bra was simple white cotton. Still, the sight of her full breasts encased in the garment was sexier than expensive lingerie would've been on someone else.

"Unhook your bra."

I swallowed a groan as she flicked open the front clasp, freeing her breasts. Her nipples were already starting to harden, the pale skin on her chest flushing.

"Now, undo my pants."

I ran my fingers through her silky curls as her hands reached for the waist of my pants. By the time she had them undone and unzipped, my cock was straining against the black cotton of my boxer briefs. Her tongue darted out, wetting her bottom lip.

"You're going to make me come," I instructed. "And you're going to swallow every last drop." I gave her curls a tug. "After all, we don't want to leave a mess for the nice steward to have to clean up, do we?"

She shook her head.

"And if you do a good job, I'll let you get yourself off

while I watch."

Her eyes widened, and she swallowed hard. I knew, for her, it would be both a punishment and a reward. This wasn't exactly public, but she knew there was always a possibility that the steward would come back in the middle of whatever we were doing. Her only other option, however, would be to suffer her arousal through the rest of the day, including meeting her parents. And I knew Hanna's appetite was such that it'd be difficult for her to just ignore it.

She reached for me, freeing my cock enough to get her mouth on it. I kept my hand on her head, but let her control the pace and depth. Sometimes I enjoyed pushing her physical limits, but right now was more about giving us both what we needed to relax and pushing her comfort limits. I wasn't into exhibitionism, and the thought of anyone getting to see Hanna in any sort of sexual manner pissed me off, but I did enjoy the thrill of the possibility.

When her mouth and tongue began to work over me, I didn't think about anything else. I closed my eyes and let my head rest against the chair. Before Hanna, I'd always thought that having a sexually experienced woman was preferable because she'd already know the best ways to give pleasure. Now, I understood the appeal of molding someone inexperienced but enthusiastic. I was the only man Hanna had ever gone down on, so I'd been able to teach her exactly what I liked.

And she was using it all now. The pressure of her tongue, the slight scrape of teeth. The amount of suction she used, and how she varied it. The way she moved her hand on the part that she couldn't take into her mouth.

It wasn't long until I was tapping her head, letting her know that I was close. I'd told her to swallow it all, but I wasn't rude enough to surprise her.

I opened my eyes as my balls tightened and the first spurt of semen raced for release. She was looking at me as I came, her gaze never leaving mine. The anxiety drained out of me as Hanna held me in her mouth, milking out every last drop, until I began to soften and the stimulation became too much.

"Your turn," I said and jerked my chin toward the chair across from me.

Flushing a pretty pink, she sat down with her legs spread, hiking her skirt up high enough for me to see everything. Her panties were soaked, and as she slid them aside, I briefly considered getting myself hard again just so I could sink into that wet heat. I dismissed the thought almost immediately though. Watching her slip two fingers into her pussy as her thumb moved over her clit was definitely turning me on, and I was pretty sure I'd be at least half-hard before she finished, but I knew that we didn't have the time for anything more.

"That's it, baby," I murmured as she arched against her hand, her breasts jutting out from her chest. "I want to see you come on your hand."

Her free hand went to her breast, fingers tugging on her nipple the way I knew she liked. She might blush, and even be a bit nervous when it came to new things, but she was never shy about enjoying sex. That was one of the things I loved the most about her. Her responses were always genuine. I never worried that she was faking or being overly enthusiastic. She let herself go when it came to sex, and she was glorious.

"Come on, baby. Let me see you come. I want those nipples hard and aching the rest of the day. I want you to feel your arousal on your thighs even as you remember the taste of me."

She bit her bottom lip as her body stiffened. Her eyes

closed, her expression going slack as she came. A shiver ran through her body as I tucked my half-erect cock back into my pants. When she was ready, I'd have her leave her panties in the bathroom with the towels. I'd be able to focus on being the perfect boyfriend if I knew my reward was having her bare underneath that skirt.

I took a slow breath. I could do this.

Chapter 4

Hanna

I'd told my parents that I was bringing my boyfriend, and I'd filled them in a bit about who he was, but that hadn't stopped them from being surprised when we pulled up to the house in our rental car. Cross had picked out one of the luxury cars, of course, so as soon as we parked, my dad and brother were checking it out. And if that wasn't enough, Mom had voiced her surprise over our timing since flights from California didn't generally get in until later. Her mouth had fallen open when Cross mentioned that we'd taken his private jet.

The rest of the night became all about grilling Cross over his family background and business practices, while still managing to slide in little digs about Juliette and me leaving the family business. And when it hadn't been those comments, it'd been about how my sister and I hadn't yet started having families, though they did congratulate me on at least having a boyfriend.

The next two days were full of similar events and conversations. Dad and RJ would take Cross to the shop and ask his opinion about various matters of business while Dad made a point of showing how skilled RJ was. Not that my brother wasn't good at his job. He'd always been mechanically inclined. I could check tire pressure, check the oil, and maybe point out a few important parts under the hood, but that was about it. I didn't look down on what my family did, but it always annoyed me when my parents felt the need to emphasis RJ's abilities while downplaying my own.

I didn't go into the shop, but rather stayed in the house with Mom and my sister-in-law as we prepared for Thanksgiving dinner. Abbie, of course, was a great cook. While she occasionally helped out with the phones and scheduling part of the business, she'd always been a housewife with intentions of becoming a stay-at-home mom. She was another case of me appreciating and respecting her choices, but my parents wouldn't stop comparing the two of us so that she came out ahead.

For example, when I told them that Cross had been teaching me to cook so I could make a side dish, Mom had given me that patronizing laugh of hers and told me not to worry about it. "Stick to what you're good at. You'd be a huge help if you just cut the vegetables for the veggie tray and made sure we have all of the condiments we need." My usual job at family gatherings. "If you think you can do that without cutting yourself."

By the time Juliette texted me to say that her flight would arrive Wednesday evening, I was all too willing to volunteer to pick her up. My parents agreed immediately. Dad and RJ would be far too busy getting things finished up at the shop so they could stay closed through the long weekend while Mom and Abbie had to finish preparations for the big meal. Cross volunteered to go with me, but when my dad asked him to stay for his and RJ's traditional excursion to the liquor store to pick out wine for tomorrow, I insisted he stay behind. He had better taste in wine and would offer to pick up the tab as his contribution to the meal, both of which I hoped would get him points with my parents.

I wasn't planning on moving back to Ohio, but I didn't want to be like Juliette either, staying away for years at a time. I wanted both my life in California and my family in Ohio. I needed my family to know how important Cross was to me, and I needed him to feel comfortable around them.

Still, it didn't stop me from wishing he was with me as I waited in the long line of cars for pick-ups. Surprisingly, my parents had let Cross and me share a room, but I was so overly conscious of being in my old bedroom that we hadn't done anything more than fall asleep next to each other. Having some alone time would've been nice. I hadn't realized how spoiled I'd been in California. With Juliette and I working together in her catering business, I was able to spend most of my free time with Cross and not feel guilty about not seeing my sister. Here, I felt like we had to constantly be doing something with one family member or another.

It was exhausting, and I was starting to understand Juliette's decision to stay away for so long.

I rubbed my temples and shifted in the seat. I'd taken the rental car instead of one of the family cars, and I had to admit that I liked the luxury. And it was nice not to feel obligated to my parents for gas or mileage or anything like that. They'd never ask me to pay for the gas, but I knew they'd hint about it in their usual passive-aggressive way.

Finally, I saw her. It wasn't until I pulled right up next to her that I realized she looked tired, and not just the kind of tired that came with a long day of travel. She looked...worn. The sort of bone-deep weariness that left lines etched on her face. Lines that hadn't been there earlier this week.

She shouldn't have changed so much in such a short period of time.

I opened my door and called her name. She looked up, her eyes wide as if I'd startled her. She grabbed her bag and came over to the car. I waited until we were heading back out of the airport before speaking.

"How was your flight?" I gave her a quick glance.

"Fine." She glanced in the visor mirror and swore. "Mom and Dad will have a field day if I show up looking like this."

She began to rummage through her purse.

"Are you okay?" I asked. "Did something happen over the last couple days?"

There was only the slightest hesitation before she shook her head. If I hadn't spent the last five months with her, I probably wouldn't have seen it. I also knew her well enough to know that she wouldn't tell me anything at the moment.

"Just the usual craziness of work," she said. "And some nerves about being here." She gave me a tight smile. "How're things going?"

I shrugged. "You know how Mom and Dad are. Asking questions about how things are going, then twisting it around so that it's all about RJ and Abbie."

Juliette sighed. "Nice to know that some things haven't changed."

"Abbie's looking good," I offered. "Two more months and the baby'll be here."

"Do they know what they're having?"

I shook my head. "They want to be surprised."

Juliette gave a sharp, brittle little laugh. "Most people would want to be prepared, you'd think."

"They did the nursery in sea foam green," I said. I

was getting some weird vibes from her, but I didn't ask. If she wanted me to know, she'd tell me when she was ready.

"Mom and Dad must be thrilled that they're finally going to be grandparents," Juliette said as she finished touching up her make-up.

"They are," I said. "Hasn't stopped them from asking when I plan to finally settle down and have kids, so be prepared."

Juliette turned to look out the window. "How's Cross handling all of it?"

"He's pretty much ignored most of it and been his usual charming self." Cross was a safe subject. "They haven't exactly said whether they like him or not, but at least their jabs have been at me. Then again, it's not like they could really find much to complain about with him. He's gorgeous, rich, and intelligent."

"You've got it bad," Juliette teased.

When I glanced at her this time, she still looked pale, and I could tell there was still something wrong, but I'd respect her clear desire not to talk about it. For the rest of the drive back to the house, we made small talk about work, about things around the apartment, a new restaurant that was opening up and whether or not we thought they'd cater enough to be competition. By the time I parked the car in the driveway, she seemed more like herself again, and I felt a bit better about the holiday going smoothly.

"Did Juliette seem off to you tonight?" I asked Cross as I settled next to him. "I mean, I knew things would be tense between her and our parents, but it felt like more than that."

He wrapped his arm around my waist as he pulled me back against him. He pressed his lips to my temple. "Think maybe she could just be airsick? I mean, she didn't eat much at dinner, did she?"

I thought for a moment and shook my head. "She didn't, and I know she loves Mom's spaghetti. I just hope she's not coming down with something. We have a couple clients coming in for meetings next week, and they specifically asked to meet with both of us."

"I hope you don't have any plans for the first day we're back." His hand slid up to cup my breast over my nightshirt. "Because I have plans for us both."

I glanced over my shoulder at him, arousal tightening things low inside me. "Oh really? And what might those plans be?"

"I haven't narrowed down all the specifics," he said, keeping his tone light, conversational. "So many options. Maybe I'll take you in every room, starting with fucking you up against the front door."

I shivered.

"Then maybe we'll move to the couch. Bend you over and take you from behind."

I liked the sound of that, and judging by the erection I could feel pressing against my ass, he liked it too.

"What next?" I asked.

"How about a round in the shower?" His fingers found my nipple. "Bodies slick and wet. Then the playroom. I think I'll tie you up, play with you a bit."

"Yes, please," I whispered. "Then what?"

30

"What do you want me to do, Hanna?" He scraped his teeth over the top of my ear. "Do you want me to fuck your ass? Your cunt? Do you want me to take you so hard that you'll feel it the next day? Spank you until it hurts to sit down?"

I growled in frustration. "Dammit, Cross. How am I ever supposed to get to sleep tonight when all I can think about is hot, kinky sex with you?"

"If it makes you feel any better, I've got a serious case of blue balls."

We both laughed, but I couldn't deny that it was a sound more of frustration than any real humor. My parents knew that Cross and I had sex. They were letting us stay in the same room. But I still couldn't bring myself to actually do anything more than cuddle and talk. No matter how badly I wanted it.

"The day we get back," I promised, "you and me, in bed all day."

"Sounds good to me," he said as his arms tightened around me.

31

Chapter 5

Cross

As the only child of two only children, holidays hadn't been about big family celebrations. We usually spend Thanksgivings at a local soup kitchen, and then went home to have our own meal before decorating the house for Christmas. Other families in our social circle hired people to come in and decorate for them, but doing it ourselves had been a tradition for as long as I could remember. We had similar traditions for other holidays too. None of them included large family gatherings.

So, when I woke on Thanksgiving morning to the smell of all sorts of wonderful things cooking, I knew I was in foreign territory. While there were only seven of us, the house somehow seemed fuller than it had before. A parade was on the television, and everyone seemed to be talking and doing stuff. Getting the meal ready. Snitching food here and there. Laughing and joking, talking about old traditions and family stories.

I heard about how, on Thanksgivings in the past, Mr. Breckenridge and the kids would play a few rounds of football before the meal and the games. They talked about a time when Mrs. Breckenridge had forgotten to get the instant mashed potatoes that everybody liked, and ended up driving to a store thirty minutes away to find them. RJ and Abbie told the story about their first Thanksgiving as a married couple and how they'd accidentally gotten things mixed up between when they were supposed to be eating with Abbie's family, so they ended up eating two meals just so no one would be upset.

It was a lot like I used to imagine holidays must've been for my friends. There had been times as a child when I wished to have what I thought of as a *normal* family, and there were a few times during the day that those feelings returned. It wasn't until later that night when I thought back over the day that I realized that things weren't as perfect as I'd thought. While Hanna's parents weren't cruel or mean, their stories, their behavior, always focused on their son. They'd said little about Juliette's success, expressed little interest in their daughters' lives other than how they reflected back on RJ. The fact that neither woman said anything about it told me that they were used to it.

I went to sleep that night wondering if having a family was worth all that drama. My own solitary Thanksgivings suddenly seemed a bit more appealing.

The day after Thanksgiving was the traditional time for the Breckenridge family to do their Christmas decorating, so I spent the entire morning and early afternoon helping RJ and Mr. Breckenridge haul giant boxes down from the attic, assisting in putting up lights and hanging decorations in the house that the women were too short to reach.

Now, I was enjoying the solitude of an empty bathroom after having taken a shower. The lack of time to myself was starting to get to me, and I was glad this was our last day here. Hanna and I would be leaving tomorrow morning, and thanks to the time difference, we'd have the rest of the day to recuperate from jet lag, then spend Sunday making up for lost time before getting back to work on Monday. While things hadn't been as bad as I'd feared they'd be, I couldn't deny that I was grateful we lived far away from Hanna's family. I couldn't have dealt with this all the time.

I ran my hand over my chin as I looked in the mirror. I'd shaved yesterday morning, but hadn't bothered yet today. There was some stubble, but I didn't think I needed to be clean-shaven at the moment, so I could pack up the toiletries I'd left in the bathroom that Hanna and I were sharing with Juliette. As I reached for my razor, my hand bumped the toothpaste, sending it right into the trashcan. Sighing, I bent over to pick it up...

And froze.

I closed my eyes, then opened them again, telling myself that I had to be seeing things.

Except I wasn't.

Right there, laying under a few bits of toilet paper, was a pregnancy test.

A *positive* pregnancy test.

I sank down to sit on the edge of the tub. My legs were numb, my stomach churning and flipping. Blood rushed in my ears.

Why hadn't Hanna told me she was pregnant? She could've taken me aside any time today. Or was she waiting until we got back to California because she didn't know how I'd react?

The questions ran circles in my head.

How had this happened? I mean, I wasn't an idiot. I knew how sex worked. But I also knew we'd always been careful. Sure, we weren't using condoms anymore, but she was on the pill and that was more effective anyway.

Or at least I'd thought it was. With other women, I'd

always worn condoms because I didn't trust that they were clean or on the pill. Maybe that was my mistake. I'd trusted Hanna to take care of things. She was responsible, organized. I never worried about her forgetting, especially since she'd been on birth control for a while.

But maybe she hadn't forgotten.

The implication of that one simple statement nearly knocked me on my ass.

Was it possible that this hadn't been an accident? Had Hanna purposefully stopped taking birth control in the hopes of getting pregnant? Men like me were great targets for that sort of thing. Women who thought that getting pregnant by a rich guy would mean enough child support to live comfortably for the next eighteen years. Or, even worse, ones who thought that a baby would automatically mean an engagement, a wedding. Women who wanted to snag a rich husband pulled that sort of shit all the time.

I'd just never thought about Hanna that way.

We'd been happy how we were. Or at least I'd thought so. Maybe I didn't know her as well as I thought I did. Her parents were clearly all about marriage and family for their girls. Maybe the pressure had been too much for her, and she'd decided this was the best way to take care of it.

The shock had started to wear off and was being replaced by both panic and anger. I clung to the latter, not wanting to give in to the former. If I did, then I'd have to start thinking about all the ways my life was about to change.

I'd never been one to shirk my responsibilities, but this was different than if we'd both forgotten to use a condom one night, or if the condom had been faulty. This wasn't even as if she'd been on something that would've nullified the birth control. She had to have done it on purpose.

All of these ugly thoughts were at the surface when the door opened.

"There you are," Hanna said.

Her bright smile, which would usually send a bolt of desire through me, just pissed me off even more.

"Mom and I–"

"When were you planning on telling me?" I cut her off, the words feeling like knives leaving my throat.

She stepped inside the bathroom and played dumb. "What are you talking about?"

"Come on, Hanna," I snapped and stood up, but kept as much distance as possible between us. "You might as well admit it. I know."

Her eyes narrowed. "I have no idea what you're talking about, and I really don't appreciate the way you're speaking to me." Her words were precise, clipped. The way she spoke when she was keeping her temper in check.

I didn't care though. All I could think about was how she'd screwed up my life.

"You're pregnant!"

Her eyes widened, and I thought I saw guilt in her surprise. "What the hell are you talking about?"

I glared down at her. Was she seriously going to play innocent here? I leaned down and pulled the test from the garbage.

"I'm not an idiot, Hanna. I know how to read these fucking things." I thrust it at her, and her eyes grew wide in horror. "When did you decide to do it? Back when we first met? After Juliette was rescued?"

"What are you talking about?" Frustration and anger and something else showed in Hanna's eyes as she folded her arms across her chest. "That isn't mine."

"Like hell it's not." I tossed it back into the trash can and washed my hands, scrubbing them as hard as possible. "You're going to tell me that it's your mom's? That it somehow magically appeared in here?" I dried my hands and crossed my own arms, not trusting myself not to hit the wall or mirror. "You really expect me to believe that you didn't purposefully get yourself pregnant so I'd marry you or so you could get money from me?"

Two spots of color appeared high on Hanna's cheeks. "Is that really what you think of me?" Her words were quiet but full of so much pain that it almost pushed away my anger.

Almost.

"Do you really think I'd do something like that? Trick you into knocking me up in the hopes you'd make a commitment? Do you think I'd actually want you that way? Forced into it?" Her eyes were shining with tears. "I'm not pregnant, Cross."

"You're lying." I looked away, focusing on the wall behind her.

"She's not."

The words came from behind me and I turned to see Juliette standing in the doorway between her room and the bathroom.

"Hanna isn't pregnant, you idiot." She glared at me. "I am."

Chapter 6

Hanna

I'd actually been enjoying the holiday, more or less. Mom and Dad were their usual selves when it came to making sure everything was done exactly how RJ liked it – the game he wanted to watch, the dishes he preferred – but that was typical for them. It was almost a Breckenridge family tradition. That they liked Cross was more important to me, and on that front, things were going well.

Then I'd stepped into the bathroom to ask Cross something, and it'd all fallen apart. He'd snapped at me, verbally attacked me, accused me not only of lying, but of trying to manipulate him by getting pregnant. I could barely believe what I was hearing, what I was seeing. This wasn't the man I'd fallen for, the man I loved. This was some angry, cruel imposter.

Then Juliette dropped the bombshell that she was pregnant.

I stepped past Cross without giving him a second look. I shoved aside all of the negative emotions I had toward him and focused on my sister. She was the one who mattered.

"Come on, Jul," I said, keeping my eyes on her.

"Let's get out of here. You and me. We'll go out, get something to eat, and you're going to talk to me."

"Hanna..."

I ignored him. I didn't want to talk to him. Didn't want to look at him. I was furious and hurt, in no position to have the sort of conversation we needed to have. I felt sick but made myself stay calm. Juliette needed my support.

And Cross could go fuck himself for all I cared at the moment.

Juliette's eyes flicked behind me, then back to me. She nodded, and I put my arm around her shoulders.

"Let's go."

Neither one of us said a word as we made our way down the stairs. Fortunately, our parents were preoccupied, and we got to the car without having to explain ourselves to anyone. She waited until we were on the road before speaking.

"I'm sorry, Hanna."

I shook my head. "Nothing to be sorry about."

"It was my test." Her voice was flat. "If I hadn't thrown it away in the bathroom, he couldn't have found it, and none of this would've happened."

"I don't want to talk about him or what he thought." I turned at the next road. "I want to talk about you."

"Not yet," Juliette said. "I need a couple minutes to get my head together."

I flicked on the radio and let Christmas music fill the car. The local station always started off on Black Friday. The traffic was surprisingly light as I made my way toward the bar and grill I liked. Most of the people in the area had probably gone to the big department stores, the places that had the big sales today. I was heading toward the section of town that had the Mom and Pop stores, the small businesses, so there was no surprise that there were only a few people out and about, bundled against the chill in the air. I didn't have any difficulties finding a parking space, which was good. I wasn't sure my frayed nerves could take any additional frustration.

Juliette and I went to a booth in the back, placed our orders, and snacked on the breadsticks until our meals came. Only after we'd taken a few bites did I broach the subject again.

"I would ask what happened, but I'm pretty sure I'd get a smart-ass response."

That earned a hint of a smile at least. "Damn straight."

I reached across the table and put my hand over hers. Her eyes met mine, and I could see the dark circles she'd tried to hide. "Talk to me."

She nodded, then took a slow breath. "I'd been getting sick in the mornings, so I suspected for a while. I just couldn't get up the nerve to take a test. But on the way to the airport, I stopped to pick up something – I don't even remember what – and bought one. I stuck it in my purse and ignored it until last night." She paused to take a gulp of water. "When I saw it, I knew I had to take it or I'd put it off forever."

"And you're pregnant," I stated the obvious.

"Looks like." She stabbed at a crouton with exceptional viciousness. "There's a chance it was a false positive, of course, but I don't think so."

"Are you late?" With our age difference, we hadn't talked a lot about personal things until I'd moved out to California. Once the whole Dominatrix thing had come out, there was very little that the two of us felt uncomfortable sharing.

"Not yet. I got one of those early detection tests

41

when I remembered Mom had morning sickness for a couple weeks before she realized she was pregnant," Juliette said. "I'll make a doctor's appointment when we get back to be sure, but I'll be shocked if I'm not."

I leaned back in my chair and let myself absorb the fact that my sister was going to have a baby. Neither of us had ever talked about kids in specific terms, but she'd always talked about her future in the singular sense. She'd dated one guy, Michael, for two months after she'd been kidnapped, but since that'd ended, she made a point of one-night stands only.

"The father...is it Michael?"

She shook her head. "I haven't been with him since we broke up."

I raised an eyebrow as I ate another fry, but I didn't ask. Now that Juliette had started, I knew she'd tell me everything.

"I'm not sure who the father is," Juliette admitted, her cheeks flushing. "I hooked up with two guys within a couple days of each other around the time I would've gotten pregnant."

"Anyone I know?"

"I doubt it," she said. "But we didn't really exchange a lot of personal information."

"What do you know about them?"

"They were Subs," she said. "The first one, I hadn't intended to sleep with. We were just going to work off some steam. Do a scene together. Things just kinda got out of hand. We used a condom, of course, but you know those things aren't always reliable."

"And the second?"

She gave me a grin this time, one that made her eyes sparkle. "Him, I definitely meant to sleep with. Again, condom. I guess the odds were against me."

42

"I thought you were on the pill."

She exhaled long and loud. "Remember that sinus infection I had?"

"Shit." I got it. "Antibiotics."

"Yup." She nodded. "I just happened to hit the right percentages all at once. Or, I guess, the wrong ones."

"Damn, Juliette." I ran my hand through my hair. "This is...wow."

"Tell me about it." She barked out a laugh. "This is the last thing I expected."

I finished my coffee, hesitated, and then asked the question I really wanted to know the answer to. "Do you know what you're going to do?"

She fell silent, her fingers moving restlessly over her utensils, then twisting her napkin.

"I don't know," she finally said. "But I won't be impulsive about it. I want to make sure that whatever I decide to do, I've thought it through."

"Will you try to find the father?"

She nodded. "I want to give him a chance to weigh in on the decision."

I reached over and squeezed her hand. "Whatever you need, I'll be there. Even if it's three a.m. feedings."

Her hand tightened around mine, and I watched her face fight for control. "Thank you."

Before either of us could say anything else, a familiar voice interrupted us.

"Hanna?"

I stiffened. I had to be hearing wrong. There was no way that voice belonged to the person I thought was standing behind me. It couldn't be him.

"Hanna Breckenridge?"

Fuck me.

I turned, feeling Juliette's eyes on me as I did so. She

43

would've heard me talk about him, but she'd moved before we'd started dating, so she wouldn't have known him by sight.

Me, on the other hand...it'd been nearly five years since we'd last seen each other, but I would've recognized Tucker Flannagan anywhere.

Hair a richer, deeper shade of blond. China blue eyes. He'd topped out at six feet tall and had put a bit more muscle on his athletic build since I'd seen him last. He'd always been good-looking and was even more so now that he'd matured a bit.

Still, I couldn't help but think that no matter how handsome Tucker was, he wasn't even close to being as attractive as Cross. His name made my heart twist painfully, and I pushed thoughts of him away.

"It is you!" Tucker beamed as he came around the table. He engulfed me in a hug, leaving me wide-eyed and feeling awkward. Then he turned to Juliette. "You have to be Hanna's sister. I heard all about you. I'm Tucker."

I saw the surprise flicker across Juliette's eyes and knew she recognized the name

"I hadn't realized you'd gotten back," he said as he pulled up a chair.

Same old Tucker.

"Juliette and I are visiting for Thanksgiving." My brain was spinning. "We're going home this weekend."

"Really?" He leaned forward, his gaze intent on me. "Where's home? I always thought you'd be at the family business, but whenever I went by, you weren't there. Your mom said you were visiting your sister."

I snorted. Leave it to my parents to call half a year a *visit*. "I went out to California after graduation to help Juliette out with her catering business, but I ended up loving it, so I took the job permanently."

"California? Wow, that's amazing!" He glanced at Juliette, then turned his attention back to me. "What is it you do?"

"We run a catering business in LA," Juliette said. "Hanna's my business manager."

"That's great, Hanna," he said with a brilliant smile. "I always knew you could do anything you set your mind to."

I gaped at him. Was this really the same man who'd slept with me right before he went away to college, then again right before he broke up with me a few months later because he couldn't handle the "long distance thing," and I hadn't wanted to transfer to Texas? He hadn't been ignorant about it, but he'd made it clear that he didn't think my degree was as important as his. Now he was acting like he'd been behind me one hundred percent.

"Look, Hanna," his tone shifted, "I know things between us ended a bit...abruptly."

I raised my eyebrows. "That's an understatement."

He had the good grace to look embarrassed. "We were kids. Let's put all that behind us, start new."

"I'm not angry, Tucker," I assured him. "I moved on a long time ago, and I'm happy."

The memory of Cross's cruel words cut through me and I pushed him from my mind. No need to bring up a relationship that I was currently pissed about.

"Besides, there's no need to be rehashing the past when we're not in town for long," I continued.

"I'm not either, actually." He moved his chair closer.

"So you don't live here?" I asked.

"I moved back after college. A lot of kids did. Finding a job isn't easy in this economy. I'm sure you understand." He straightened. "I'm so excited to hear that you live in California now. It'll be great to know someone there. I'm moving to LA in a couple days."

Chapter 7

Cross

The moment I heard Juliette say that the test was hers, I felt like an idiot. It was the most logical explanation, and I hadn't even thought of it. Then again, neither had Hanna, and Juliette was her sister. It made sense that I'd forgotten about her, forgotten that she was sharing the bathroom with us, but this was Hanna's childhood home. She'd shared this bathroom with Juliette for years. All she'd needed to do was tell me that it was probably her sister's test, and it would've diffused the entire situation.

Instead, she'd acted like I was behaving irrationally. Like I hadn't had every reason in the world to be freaking out. She knew I didn't want kids now. Maybe ever. I wasn't thinking that far ahead. I liked things the way they were. Liked how the two of us were together.

But as much as I kept telling myself that Hanna should've stopped all of this from happening, I couldn't stop the guilt that came when I saw the hurt on her face. She wasn't just angry with me. She was upset, and when I thought of some of the things I'd said to her, I couldn't really blame her. I had been a little harsh.

"Hanna."

She didn't even acknowledge me as she went to her sister. And then they were gone. It didn't hit me until they'd reached the stairs that I needed to go after Hanna. She couldn't just leave without us working it out. I couldn't have her upset with me the rest of the day.

I went after her then, but it was too late. Hanna had taken the car, and I had no idea where she and her sister had gone.

"Is something wrong?" The sister-in-law, Abbie, came up behind me.

I glanced over at her, my stomach twisting as I watched her run her hand over her stomach. Hanna said the baby was due next month. Maybe that was why I'd freaked out so badly. Seeing how Hanna's family had been about the upcoming baby, it must've made me think that was what she wanted. Once I explained that to Hanna, I was sure she'd understand.

"Hanna and Juliette left but didn't tell me where they were going." I kept my voice even.

Abbie was nice enough. Sweet, cute. Chestnut curls. Hazel eyes. She looked like the stereotypical Midwestern housewife. She fit here, with the Breckenridge family, with their auto business and holiday traditions. I could see, though, why Juliette didn't. Hanna, I wasn't so sure of. While she wasn't quite jaded enough for Hollywood, she didn't quite seem to fit here either.

"Do you think they might've gone shopping?" Abbie asked. "There are always some good Black Friday deals at the shopping mall."

"I don't think so," I muttered.

I looked down the driveway. Hanna had taken the rental, so if I planned to go after her, I would need to borrow another vehicle. I looked with distaste at the pair of ancient cars sitting there. I was sure they ran well.

After all, that wouldn't have been very good for business. It didn't make them any more appealing though.

"What's everyone looking at?" RJ was suddenly there, grinning that wide grin of his. His hair was the same color as Juliette's, but his eyes were blue rather than violet, and his features were a bit harsher, but the resemblance was there.

"Hanna and Juliette went somewhere, and Cross was wondering if anyone knew where," Abbie supplied.

I wondered if she always sounded so cheery, and if she did, how in the world her husband stood it. I mean, I wouldn't want to be around someone who was a bitch all the time, but that constant bubbly personality would grate on my nerves after a while.

Then again, for all I knew, any woman would eventually get on my nerves. Being with Hanna was the longest I'd ever been in a relationship, and I had no idea how much longer it would last.

And I had a bad feeling that if I didn't make things right with Hanna sooner rather than later, what we had wouldn't be around much longer.

I looked up at RJ. I was tall, but he was at least six and a half feet. "Would you happen to know where Hanna and Juliette might be?"

RJ shrugged. "Whenever Hanna was home from college, she used to go to Hanson Bar and Grill off Main Street. Maybe they went there."

That made sense. Hanna wanted to talk to Juliette, find out what was going on, and I was sure she wouldn't want her family accidentally overhearing. That sounded like the perfect place for a private conversation.

"Excuse me." I left RJ and Abbie as I headed toward the kitchen where I could hear Mrs. Breckenridge singing. Despite how much I disliked how the

49

Breckenridge parents put their daughters in the backseat, they were overall good people.

"Mrs. Breckenridge."

She looked up. The first couple days, she and her husband had tried to get me to call them Raymond and Caroline, but I'd stuck with the more formal address. I said it was because I wanted to be polite, respectful, but I knew that a deep part of me felt like if I called them by their first names, it'd mean something more.

"Hi, Cross." She smiled at me, the resemblance to her daughters making my heart give a painful thump. "Is there something I can do for you?"

"Actually, ma'am, I was wondering if I could borrow a car? Hanna and Juliette took the rental."

"Of course." She gestured toward a bowl next to the back door. "Grab a set of keys. Both cars should have full tanks."

I fished out one and headed outside. The car door wasn't even locked. Some people might've liked the whole small town vibe they had going on, but I had a feeling I'd get stir-crazy before too long.

I pulled up my GPS and typed in the information to get the directions I needed. A few minutes later, I was on my way.

The entire drive, I thought about what I was going to say, how I could convince her that this was all just some vast misunderstanding. She had to know that sort of thing was a man's worst nightmare. Not a baby in and of itself. One that was planned for, a wanted part of a family, that was cause for celebration. A surprise after less than six months of dating – that was cause for freaking out. Any other man would've been just as pissed if they'd thought their girlfriend had tricked them.

I passed by a dozen little shops, then nearly slammed

on my brakes when I saw the jewelry store. It wasn't some name brand place, but it looked nice enough to find what I wanted.

They were open, of course. After all, it was Black Friday. The resemblance between the two gentlemen behind the counter left no doubt to their relation, though they were both of such an indiscriminate age that it was difficult to say if they were father and son or brothers.

"Good afternoon, sir." The older of the two spoke first. "How may we help you?"

"I'm looking for something for my girlfriend." I walked past the case of rings to the one holding the necklaces and bracelets. "Something, I think, in silver."

I'd had Hanna's collar specially made. Before her, I'd never thought I'd want a woman enough to make that sort of commitment, but when I realized that I wanted to stake a claim on her, I'd been very particular. I wouldn't find anything of quite so fine a quality here, but I was hopeful I'd find something that could help smooth the way for me.

"We have a lovely selection." The younger one moved to stand across from me. "Are you looking for anything with stones, or purely metal?"

I looked down at the bracelets, my gaze sliding from one with rubies to one with diamonds. Then I saw it. Amethyst. A couple were deep purple, but there was one with paler stones, almost the color of Hanna's eyes.

"That one." I pointed at it.

The man reached inside and pulled out the bracelet I was looking at. "A lovely choice, sir. Very high quality."

I lifted it, turning it this way and that. I wasn't a professional, but I considered myself to have a good eye. If I'd been home, I would've taken it to a jeweler friend of mine to ensure that I was seeing it correctly, but right now, I'd take the chance. Besides, these two didn't look like the kind to swindle anyone.

"I'll take it." I handed the bracelet back to the young man. "Wrap it nicely, please."

"Yes, sir." The younger man handed the bracelet off to the older man and then took my card.

Five minutes later, I was back in the car, this time with a beautifully wrapped box sitting on the passenger's seat. I wasn't foolish enough to think I could actually buy Hanna's forgiveness, but a nice gift never hurt.

I resumed my drive, and as I turned into the parking lot, I spotted the rental. I pulled up next to it, but didn't get out yet. I still wasn't entirely sure what to say to Hanna, especially since her sister was with her. I could probably get Juliette to give us some privacy, but I also wasn't selfish enough to think that Juliette needed Hanna right now less than I did. I considered Juliette a friend, so I did feel for her too.

Being there for Juliette would actually be a good way to show Hanna that I wasn't a complete ass, I realized. We'd be part of what Juliette was going through when we went back home, so I might as well start now.

With a plan solidly in place, I felt a bit more confident that I could handle the situation, and that was what I needed, to feel in control. I wasn't as much of a total control freak as some Dominants who had to have every single thing exactly perfect or they freaked out, but I was enough about control that I wanted a plan, a schedule, specific points to follow.

I put the box in my jacket pocket and then got out of the car. As I walked toward the door, I glanced in one of the large windows as I passed...just in time to see a good-looking blond man hug my girlfriend.

I stopped, watched, waited to see how Hanna would react.

But she didn't shove the man away. Instead, she smiled at him. Let him sit down next to her.

One little fight and she was acting like she wasn't mine. Like the collar I'd given her didn't mean anything. That the last five months and all we'd done together didn't mean anything.

The man looked too familiar with her, too comfortable being close to her. And she wasn't putting distance between them, not even when he leaned toward her. I couldn't watch to see what happened next.

As soon as I got in the car, I pulled out my phone. I'd hired this particular pilot to fly Hanna and me here because he had no plans for the holiday, and had been more than happy to accept the rather large bonus I'd offered for him to be on call. He answered right away, and I made a mental note to add a bit more to his bonus for actually doing what he was supposed to.

By the time I dropped off the car and called in a taxi, I received a text saying that the plane would be ready to take off by the time I arrived at the airfield. I made a vague excuse to the Breckenridges, then carried my bag out to the taxi. I gave the address and didn't look back as the car pulled away.

I didn't want to see this place ever again. In fact, I was pretty sure I didn't want to see anyone from this family either.

I was going home.

Chapter 8

Hanna

It was getting close to eight o'clock by the time Juliette and I arrived back at our parents' house. Tucker had hung around for at least an hour, talking about how he'd gotten a degree in finance but had decided that he didn't want to be an accountant. According to him, LA was the place to be for a fresh start. I hadn't really minded catching up with him, but between Juliette's announcement and my fight with Cross, I'd barely listened to anything Tucker had to say.

As I parked the car, Juliette asked, "Why didn't you tell Tucker that you were seeing someone?"

I looked over at her. "I didn't really think about it," I lied. "Besides, after the shit Cross said to me, I don't know how true that's going to be."

Even as I said it, I felt sick to my stomach. Every couple argued, but the things he'd said had been awful. For me, it was as bad as if he'd accused me of infidelity. It hadn't been a miscommunication. The fact that he'd thought I could be that devious spoke volumes. He clearly didn't know me as well as I thought he did, and he didn't trust me. That's what hurt the most. When I was at my most vulnerable, I'd put my life and well-being in his hands. I'd let him introduce me to a work where trust was key.

And he'd proven that it only went one way with us.

Juliette reached over and put her hand on my arm. "I've got your back, no matter what happens."

I gave her a weak smile. She was the one who needed support right now, not me, but I was grateful to have her. With our age difference, we hadn't been particularly close growing up. She'd been my babysitter, but she'd been gone by the time I was a teenager. It'd only been over the last year that the two of us had truly become friends. More than ever, I was grateful I'd gone to California.

"Don't tell Mom and Dad," Juliette said. "About the baby. We both know they'll assume I'm keeping it, and then try to convince me to move back here."

She was right. While I was pretty sure she would at least have the baby, I knew the odds of her keeping it was about fifty-fifty. The one thing she'd never do, though, was come back to Ohio. At least with me in California with her, our parents couldn't say she had no family.

"I won't say anything," I promised. "And I'll have your back whatever you decide to do."

We stayed there in silence for a minute and then got out of the car. RJ and Abbie must've already gone home for the night because only our parents were sitting in the living room, watching the first of dozens of Christmas specials I knew they'd be watching over the next few weeks. Another Breckenridge family tradition.

"Where did you two run off to?" Mom asked, glancing away from the screen for a minute to look at us.

"Just wanted to see the town," I said. "See if anything changed. We stopped by the bar and grill to get something to eat. Took a look at some of the shops."

"You know, Hanna, The Honey Tree has been looking for a new manager," Mom said. "I know you've never been interested in the auto business, but you always liked that little place. I'll bet Mrs. Franco would love to take you on."

I forced a smile even as the muscles in my jaw clenched. "Thanks, Mom, but Juliette and I work well together. I really enjoy what I do."

Both parents looked up this time, and I felt Juliette stiffen next to me. I resisted the urge to reach over and squeeze her hand. She didn't need me acting like she needed reassurance while our parents were right there.

"I know, sweetie," Mom continued. "It's just when I think of the two of you scraping by, sharing an apartment..."

Out of the corner of my eye, I saw Juliette scowl, and something in me snapped. "Actually, Juliette's place is over twelve hundred square feet. We each have our own bedroom and bathroom, and the view is gorgeous. It's a lot less crowded than you'd think." I gave my parents a saccharine sweet smile. "As for us scraping by, I doubt Mrs. Franco would be able to match my salary and health benefits."

Juliette covered a laugh with a cough.

"I appreciate you looking out for us," I said. "I promise, if we're ever in trouble, we'll let you know."

Juliette and I both knew that wasn't entirely true. When she was kidnapped over the summer, I'd waited until she been found before letting our parents know what happened, and even then, we'd given them a sanitized version, downplaying the danger Juliette had been in. And, of course, we hadn't said a word about how she'd known the male kidnapper. While the catering company did do well, our parents could never know that Juliette supplemented her income by being a Dominatrix at a local club.

"I'm tired," Juliette said. "And my flight leaves fairly early, so I'm going to head up to bed."

"Me too," I said, following her as my stomach began to churn.

Cross and I hadn't decided yet when we were leaving, but now that I was back, I knew that he and I needed to talk. Since he wasn't with my parents, he was most likely in bed, still stewing over how we'd left things. Hopefully, he already realized how out of line he was and would apologize right away. It'd make things much easier to hash out once that was done, and I didn't want this to follow us back to California. If we were going to work this out, I wanted to do it here and forget about it.

If.

The word made my heart ache. I didn't want it to be *if.* I wanted it to be *when.* And I wanted that to be now.

But I wasn't going to just let him off without talking about what happened, what it meant. He'd been disrespectful and mean, and I couldn't let that go.

Juliette gave me a sympathetic look as she stopped at her bedroom door, and I took a deep breath.

As soon as I opened my old bedroom door, I frowned. Cross wasn't there. I walked over to the bathroom door, but didn't need to knock. It was partially open...and empty. I turned again to look at my room, a feeling of unease settling in my stomach. Something was wrong, and it took me a moment to figure out what it was.

The shorts he'd worn to bed were gone. I walked over to the closet and opened it. His suitcase, and all the clothes he'd hung in the closet were gone as well. I didn't need to look in the dresser to confirm my suspicion, but I did it anyway. Empty.

Emotions came at me, one after the other. Shock that he'd left. Hurt that he hadn't called.

I pulled my phone from my pocket and confirmed that I hadn't missed any calls. Or texts. Or anything that indicated Cross had tried to contact me to tell me which emergency had sent him back to the West Coast so quickly.

With that realization, anger overcame the other emotions, and my hands shook.

He left. We had a fight, and instead of sticking around to work things out, he ran like a child. No note, no call.

"Cowardly bastard," I muttered and slammed the bathroom door. "Son of a bitch!"

"Hanna?" Juliette opened the door I'd just closed. "What's wrong?" She looked around. "Where's Cross?"

"That would be what's wrong." I took a shaky breath. "He's not here."

There was a moment of silence, and then Juliette shook her head and spoke again, "He has to be. I'm sure he's somewhere."

"His things are gone."

Juliette's mouth took on a familiar stubborn set. "Let's go see what our parents say."

Heat flooded my face. "I don't want to get them involved."

"Come on." She took my arm and the two of us went downstairs. Our parents looked up in surprise, but she spoke before they could. "Did Cross go somewhere? We can't seem to find him."

Dad shrugged and turned his attention back to the television even as he answered, "He said he was being called away. I'm surprised he didn't call you."

My nails dug into my palm. "He didn't. Thank you."

I turned and practically ran back up the stairs. I heard Juliette following, but I closed the door. I didn't want to talk to her at the moment. I wanted Cross. And that was the problem. When I was upset, he calmed me, soothed me. He was the one who'd taken care of me when Juliette had been kidnapped. He'd made sure I was safe, protected me.

I never thought I'd need to be protected from him.

I laid down on the bed, phone in hand, and debated about calling him. I was torn between wanting to hear his voice and not wanting to make the first move. He'd been the one who'd done wrong. It shouldn't have been up to me to try to make things right.

But I had to respond. I couldn't let him think that I hadn't even noticed he was gone. I wouldn't do that to him. And, if I was being completely honest, I didn't want to give him the satisfaction of knowing how badly he'd hurt me.

After forcing myself to think things through, I wrote out a text. Then re-read it to make sure I wasn't sending out some emotional shit that could come back to bite me in the ass. I had to be an adult about this. Communicate.

Call me when you land. I don't want to have this conversation over the phone, but I need to know you've arrived safely, and we need to set up a time to talk when I get back.

I didn't expect an immediate response if for no other reason than Cross was in the air now, but I couldn't stop looking at my phone. I forced myself into the bathroom, into the shower. I resisted the urge to hurry, to run back to my phone and see if he'd texted while I was gone. But by the time I was done, there was still no response. I didn't know exactly when he left, but I reminded myself it was highly possible he hadn't gotten back yet.

And I kept telling myself that until well past midnight. Even if Cross had left shortly before Juliette and I had gotten back, the plane should've landed. It was a four and a half hour flight. I then started to tell myself that he might not have checked his phone right away.

When I woke up just before dawn, however, I saw that my message hadn't only been delivered, but that it'd been read too. He was ignoring me. I squeezed my eyes closed even though I knew I wouldn't get back to sleep. I pressed my hands to my chest, trying to fight the rising nausea. He wasn't even going to give me the courtesy of a reply.

I could feel the tears coming and pressed my face into the pillow. I couldn't stop them, but I could keep anyone else from hearing them. When I finally stopped and raised my head, the sun still wasn't up, but there was a message on my phone.

It was from Juliette.

I managed to get you a seat on my flight if you're coming back to LA.

Right. Because I didn't have a return ticket. I hadn't thought I'd need one. I'd come on a private plane with Cross and planned on returning with him.

Now I had to decide if I wanted to return at all.

I put my hands over my eyes. I'd been there before, wondering if I should stay in LA or stay where it was safe and let my parents take care of me. They would, I knew. I could go downstairs and tell them that I'd made a mistake, that I wanted to come home. They'd let me live here until I earned enough money to get my own place.

And they'd never let me forget how I'd screwed up, how I'd failed. They'd constantly be there, telling me how to live my life, how I was disappointing them.

I'd lose the freedom I found in LA, lose my

friendships. I'd lose a job that I cared about and enjoyed. And I'd be leaving behind a sister who needed me now more than ever. No matter what happened with Cross, I couldn't leave Juliette.

I refused to let a man chase me from my home and my family.

I got up and headed for the closet. I'd need to get dressed and pack quickly if I was going to make the flight.

Home wasn't Zanesville, Ohio, not anymore. And LA wasn't home because of Cross. It was where I belonged.

And I was going home.

Chapter 9

Hanna

I took an extra dose of Dramamine so I could sleep for the whole flight home. I did it as much for Juliette as for myself. I didn't want to talk about any of it and she had enough on her mind than to worry about what I was going through, but I knew she'd try to help anyway. So I slept, and she got to spend the trip thinking about whatever it was she needed to think about.

Thanks to the time difference, we got back to California when it was still morning, but I knew better than to try to find Cross right away. When I told Juliette that I was going back to the apartment with her, she told me that she thought it was a good idea.

"I'm surprised," I said as we went to the baggage claim to get my luggage. "I would've thought you'd be encouraging me to go fix things. I thought you liked Cross."

Juliette followed me to the taxi line. "I do," she said. "But I only like him for how the two of you are together. He fucked that up, so I'm with you."

I swallowed hard and spoke past the lump in my throat, "Thank you."

The next morning, I considered calling first, but since Cross hadn't answered any of my previous attempts at contact, I doubted today would be any different. I did send off a text so I wouldn't completely surprise him, but there wasn't any response.

I had a key, but I knocked on the door instead. After what happened, I wasn't so sure I'd be welcome coming in as if I had the right to be there. It wasn't my home, no matter how much time I'd spent there over the last few months. When no one answered, I relented and used the key. If Cross wasn't there, I'd get some of my things and leave him a note telling him that I was done trying to reach out to him.

When I stepped into the living room, however, Cross was there.

He was sprawled out on the couch, wearing only a pair of sweatpants. His hair was a mess, and when his eyes flicked up to me, they were bloodshot. I didn't need to smell the reek of alcohol to know he was drunk. The half dozen empty bottles scattered around told me all I needed to know.

"Hanna." He slurred my name as he forced himself up into a sitting position. "You're here."

All of the things I'd thought about saying, the questions I wanted to ask, moved to the background as anger came forward.

"What the hell is wrong with you?" I snapped. "Seriously, Cross, have you lost your ever-fucking mind?!"

He frowned as he tried to stand, stumbled, then

managed to get to his feet. "You don't need to yell. And I don't need to explain myself to you. This is my house and I'll get drunk if I want to."

I wanted to tell him he sounded like a petulant child, but I wasn't about to pick a new fight when we already had one we needed to resolve.

"I wanted to talk to you," I said. "But I can't when you're like this."

He snorted and grabbed a bottle from the floor. "Thought you would've gotten the hint by now. I don't want to talk to you."

My eyes burned, but I refused to give in to tears. Instead, I pulled my anger closer and used it to keep myself focused.

"I just wanted some time to myself. I mean, we just spent a week non-stop together. It was fucking claustrophobic." He took a drink from the bottle. "I don't think it's too much to ask to be left alone for a few days."

"That's what you want?" I curled my hands into fists. My entire body shook with anger. "You accuse me of being manipulative, among other things, and when you've been proven wrong, you run away."

He glared down at me. "What was I supposed to think?"

"What were you supposed to think?" I barked out a bitter laugh. "How about you were supposed to *trust* me?!"

He shrugged and staggered over to the window. "Trust you? That's a laugh."

"Excuse me?" I moved forward a few steps. "You were the one who told me our entire relationship was based on trust. And I trusted you."

He grimaced as he glanced over his shoulder. "Spare me the self-righteous shit."

"I'm not pregnant, you asshole!" I'd never been a violent person, but right now, I wanted to slap him. "I never was! So I didn't lie! I didn't trick you or any of the other shit you accused me of! I didn't do anything wrong!"

"Why didn't you just tell me that it was Juliette's?" he asked. "I mean, you're so smart. You should've figured it out. It's not like you forgot she was there."

I stared at him, hardly believing what I was hearing. Was he seriously going to blame me for what happened? Sure, in the heat of the moment, I'd forgotten that Juliette was sharing a bathroom with us, but that was hardly reason to blame me. Just because I hadn't been able to come up with a different person to blame, an explanation that made sense, didn't mean his behavior was justified.

"It shouldn't matter if there wasn't another explanation. It shouldn't matter if the evidence pointed to what you thought." I took a step toward him. "You should've trusted me."

He turned, his eyes blazing. "*Trusted* you? Sure, Hanna, I should've trusted you."

His words were still blunted, but his anger seemed to be sobering him enough to get out what he needed to say.

"I went after you," he continued. "That day. I went after you so we could talk." He gestured toward a box sitting on the coffee table. "Bought you a gift, even."

What was he talking about?

"I went to that restaurant. Saw you there, with that guy."

For a moment, I had no clue who he was talking about. Then it hit me. Tucker.

"He looked like he knew you real well."

I folded my arms. "Yes, he did. We grew up together."

Cross's laugh was brittle. "I'm sure you two were good friends. Did you have fun *catching up*?"

"Actually, we did, asshole. Unlike *some* people, Tucker can actually manage polite conversation without accusing me of being a horrible person."

Cross's eyes narrowed. "Tucker. As in your ex-boyfriend who fucked you then dumped you? No wonder he looked *familiar* with you. Did the two of you get *reacquainted* now that you've gotten some experience under your belt?"

"You bastard."

He drained the last of the amber liquid from the bottle.

"I trusted you to take care of me." My voice trembled, but I forced myself to say it all. "I believed in you. Took you home to meet my family–"

"There was your first mistake," he cut me off, "thinking I wanted anything to do with your family. Or any family for that matter."

I flinched and hated myself for it. I couldn't help it though. Everything I thought we were moving toward, he didn't want, had never wanted. He'd called me his lover, his girlfriend, but I assumed that meant we would eventually become more, that we'd have a family together. I never once considered that my fears had been right, that he didn't want a future with me.

Now, however, I could see that I should've listened to my sister after all. She'd warned me to stay away from him. For the first time, I regretted that I hadn't.

"I wish I'd never met you."

I turned and walked away, half-hoping he'd come after me, tell me that he hadn't meant any of it, that he was just scared that he might lose me. All of the things the heroes in romance novels did when they realized their woman was walking away.

But he didn't.

I managed to hold back the tears until the taxi dropped me off in front of Juliette's apartment building, but they started to flow the moment I stepped inside. I could barely see or breathe when I walked into the apartment, and then Juliette's arms were around me, and she held me as my heart broke, as my world fell apart.

Chapter 10

Cross

I let the water beat down on me, and closed my eyes, knowing I would have a hell of a hangover once this was all done, but the pain that would come with sobriety, I knew, would be worse. I started drinking as soon as I'd gotten on the plane, and I hadn't stopped since. Whenever I felt the buzz fading, I found more to drink. By the time Hanna surprised me at home, I'd made my way through most of the alcohol I had in the place. The only thing I hadn't touched was the wine, and that was because it didn't do anything to help me forget. I needed something stronger for that.

Now, with Hanna's last words ringing in my head, I knew there wasn't enough booze in the world to make things better.

I wish I'd never met you.

The pain knifed through me each time I remembered the expression on her face, the venom in her words. I wished the alcohol could make me forget what I said to her. All those horrible, awful things that I never thought I could ever say to anyone, much less the woman I loved.

And that's what made this so much worse than anything I'd ever done before. I loved her. For a while I thought that was all that mattered. Then, when she'd asked me to meet her family, I'd thought it was just about making her happy. I'd been nervous, of course, but it wasn't until I'd seen that pregnancy test that it hit me all at once. It didn't matter how much I loved Hanna. I had my life, and I was happy with it. I didn't want anything else.

Except I didn't have Hanna now.

She walked out, said that she wished she'd never met me.

I didn't know how to handle this. In the past, I'd had sexual partners who'd gotten too attached, and I'd had to make sure they understood I wasn't interested in anything long-term. It'd been so long since I'd cared about anyone for more than just sex that I'd forgotten what it was like to deal with real feelings.

"Fuck it all," I muttered as I climbed out of the shower.

Hanna had left. She didn't want to see me again, wished that she'd never seen me in the first place. She hadn't given me a chance to really explain how panicked I'd been, why I'd acted the way I had. She hadn't even tried to understand what I'd been going through.

But that nagging little voice in the back of my head told me that no matter how much Hanna had yelled at me, no matter what she'd said, none of this was her fault. I was the one who overreacted, no matter my reasons. I'd left before we could talk, didn't let her explain what happened with the man at the bar and grill.

Tucker.

I ground my teeth together. She'd told me about him when we'd first gotten together. Before me, the only man she'd ever slept with had been her high school sweetheart, and they'd only done it twice. I hadn't really thought about him since then. He hadn't left much of an impression on her, and I'd believed the things we'd done together had long since made her forget that she'd ever been with anyone else.

I caught a glimpse of my reflection in the mirror and scowled. I smelled better now, but that was pretty much the lone improvement. I looked like shit.

I needed to get out of here, find something else to distract me from drinking myself into a stupor. Again. I had to go back to work tomorrow, and I was already going to have a hell of a hangover. I didn't need to do anything to make it worse. I needed to get out tonight.

There was one place I knew that would give me the distraction I needed. I hadn't been there without Hanna since we'd first gotten together, but it was the place I'd gone to relax for years, and if I ever needed that, it was now.

Sunday evenings at the club were fairly quiet, and the one after Thanksgiving was even more so. Still, there were always a handful of people who managed to make it in, so when I walked into the club, I wasn't alone. These were the people I'd always been the most open with, the ones who understood the sorts of things that most people didn't get.

The music seemed louder than usual, but I was glad. The pounding rhythm helped keep my mind from wandering, gave me something else to focus on. I went to the bar and ordered Highland Park Scotch. One of the best things about this club was the wide selection of beverages to choose from. They had a stricter policy on liquor due to the nature of the club, but the quality more than made up for it.

"Cross!"

I looked over as a familiar couple came over.

Miranda and Jason had been together for more than a year, both in and out of the club. She was a Dominatrix, and he was her Sub, but they were more than just that. I'd seen them together a few times in public, looking as a normal as the next couple.

Miranda was short and slender, with honey-colored curls, and one of those perpetually youthful faces. She was a librarian at one of the area high schools. Jason barely looked old enough to be out of high school, but I knew he was a grad student working on his thesis. Some sort of biology or physics or something like that.

They were good together, in and out of the club. Part of me wanted to ask them how they did it, how they managed a balance between what they were here and who they were in the real world. Instead, I smiled and raised my glass.

"It's good to see you," Miranda raised her voice to be heard over the music.

Jason simply nodded, but I hadn't expected him to answer. He was already wearing a gag.

"Nice to see you too," I said. "You two look good together."

They were wearing matching outfits of red leather that complemented their different colorings. Miranda's dress stopped just below her ass, and the neckline plunged to her navel. Jason was wearing a pair of leather pants that I was sure would be a bit uncomfortable by the end of the night if he didn't get any release. And with Miranda, it was fifty-fifty that he'd get it.

"Where's Hanna?" Miranda looked around, clearly expecting to see the other woman appear at my side.

There was a conversation I didn't want to have with anyone, especially not like this.

"Are you two performing today?" I asked as I set my

glass on the counter.

Miranda smiled. "We are, actually. Are you and Hanna ever going to get up and show us what you've got?"

I shook my head, my jaw clenched so tight that it actually hurt. I hoped they'd see it as a possessive Dom not wanting to share his Sub, as someone who wasn't fond of exhibitionism. I might enjoy some voyeurism, but even if Hanna had been here, my answer still would've been no. The thought of anyone else seeing Hanna naked, seeing her come, pissed me off.

Except if things between us were truly and fully broken, someone else would see her naked, see her come. Even if she didn't stay in the BDSM world, she'd find a boyfriend. No other man might get to know what it was like to see her submit, to know what it was like to have her complete surrender, but they would get to know the feel of her lips around their cock, the heat of her tight pussy.

The realization made me sick.

I didn't notice that Miranda and Jason had left until I heard them being announced. I looked up at the stage, a strange wave of deja vu washing over me as I remembered that Miranda and Jason had performed the first night I brought Hanna here.

I pushed aside the memory and focused on the couple on stage. I'd wanted a distraction. Miranda and Paul were a good way to get it without having to try to muster up the energy to find a Sub. Hell, I wasn't even sure I could manage to get it up. Between the alcohol and my conflicting feelings about Hanna, my body probably wouldn't respond the way I'd want it to. Or maybe I didn't want to, and that's the reason I decided to stay on the bar stool and watch instead of going over to talk to one of the

73

women who kept sending looks my way.

Miranda led Jason across the stage to where a padded bench had been set up. She moved with a brisk efficiency, slipping Jason's hands into the leather restraints on either side of the bench, then tightened them. Once they were in place, she removed the gag and gave Jason a sip of water from a bottle.

Sometimes the lead-up was almost as good as the scene itself. There were all sorts of ways things could go, and it was always fun to imagine what was coming next. I'd seen Miranda and Jason together enough to know that whatever they did would be good.

The music dropped to a low beat that kept the place from being silent, but would still allow us to hear every moan and cry.

Miranda moved in front of Jason and reached down to grab his hair. She used it to tilt his head back as she moved to stand over him.

"Make me come." She didn't shout, but she'd performed enough to know how to perfectly project her voice so we could all hear her.

His face disappeared between her legs, and she began to moan. Blood rushed to my cock, but it wasn't because of what I was seeing. It was because I was thinking of how Hanna sounded when I went down on her. The taste of her on my tongue.

I must've been lost in memories for a few minutes, because the next thing I knew, Miranda was crying out her pleasure as Jason completed the task she'd set before him. He panted as she stepped back, his shoulders heaving with each breath he took.

She walked around behind him, her skin flushed, but otherwise seemingly unaffected. She reached around and unfastened the front of Jason's pants, then tugged them down to his thighs. A shudder went through him when Miranda swung the cane she held, but I knew Jason well enough to know it was anticipation rather than dread. He liked a fair bit more pain than I was comfortable with, but that was why he was with Miranda. Subs found Dominants who matched them, who gave them what they needed. Most people thought that all Submissives, all Dominants, were the same, but the tastes were as varied among those in this lifestyle as there were in others.

The sharp sound of the cane on flesh echoed in the room, mingled with Jason's moans and cries. His skin reddened until I knew he would be bruised in the morning, no matter how well Miranda took care of him after, but he kept thanking her, begging for more.

The palm of my hand tingled as I thought of the times I'd spanked Hanna, felt her skin warm. I remembered how much she'd trusted me to let her do that, to show her how a little pain could intensify pleasure. My gut churned, and I forced my attention back to the scene playing out on stage.

Miranda had put the cane down, and was now standing behind Jason, her fingers between his cheeks. None of us had to see graphic details to know what she was doing. Her arm moved back and forth even as Jason rocked back against her hand, moaning, begging for her to touch his cock.

"No, baby," she said in a chiding voice. "You have to come just from my fingers in your ass."

I clenched my hand into a fist, remembering the first time I'd breached Hanna's ass with my fingers. She might not have been a virgin when we met, but she'd been almost as inexperienced as one, and I'd loved knowing that I was the first person to touch her there, the first one to fuck her that way.

And now, unless something changed, I'd never do it again. I'd gone with her to Ohio with every intention of keeping our relationship as solid as it had been these past few months. Instead, it had all fallen apart, and I didn't know what to do to fix it.

If it could be fixed at all.

Chapter 11

Hanna

I blinked as a drop of liquid ran down my cheek, then turned the eye dropper to the other eye. When I lowered my head, I reached for a towel and wiped the drops from my cheeks before I faced my reflection. My eyes were still blood-shot, the skin around them swollen and red, but the eye drops had helped some. Still, nothing would completely wipe away the evidence of what happened yesterday.

I sighed and began to apply cover-up to the raw skin. I couldn't remember the last time I'd cried so much or so often. When Juliette had been kidnapped, I hadn't really cried that much, but yesterday, I hadn't been able to stop. Every hurtful thing Cross had said to me over the past couple days replayed over and over again, sparking a fresh round of tears each time. There was anger beneath the pain, and it was the anger that had given me the strength to get out of bed this morning.

I gave myself one last look to confirm that I'd done the best I could, and then walked out to join Juliette. Neither one of us said anything as we headed for the elevator. I hadn't wanted to tell her what happened, but she'd taken me to my room and refused to leave until I'd told her every last detail.

It'd actually felt better once I'd gotten it all out, though I believed it was due more to the fact that my sister had been furious on my behalf rather than any sort of catharsis that came with the retelling. Juliette had paced and cursed and threatened to castrate, then disemboweled Cross for being such a jerk. I knew she wouldn't really resort to violence, but it was nice to have the support. It was also comforting to know that I wasn't overreacting. I hadn't admitted it until that moment that part of what was worrying me was fear that I'd been blowing it all out of proportion, that any of the points Cross had made were valid. Juliette had assured me that wasn't the case.

"I ended up giving everyone Wednesday and Friday off too." Juliette broke the silence. "So there's only two days' worth of billing to go through."

I nodded, following her outside into the warm California sunshine. While Zanesville wasn't as snowy or cold as northern Ohio, this much sun definitely wasn't what I was used to in December. For once, I almost wished it was overcast and miserable so it would match the way I felt. Logically, I knew that the weather wouldn't make me feel any better, but that didn't stop me from feeling like the bright blue sky was mocking me.

"The Nelson luncheon on Thursday is minimal work," Juliette continued. "They ended up deciding that they only wanted the food brought in, so there aren't any logistics to worry about with wait staff."

"And the Breashears' brunch is Saturday, right?" I asked. I was pretty sure that was when it'd been scheduled, but talking over things helped me focus on the work ahead of me rather than everything else.

"At eleven," Juliette confirmed. "Missie asked that we be set up by ten forty-five and that you and I meet with her at ten."

A weird sensation of déjà vu washed over me. I'd been working a dinner for Missie Breashears the first time I met Cross, even though it wasn't the same sort of event. Juliette hadn't been able to make it to the party, thanks to her former assistant cutting her brake lines, so

I'd played hostess. A few people had mistaken me for her, including Cross.

With the memory came a question I hadn't let myself consider since those first few days together. Cross had approached me, thinking I was Juliette, a Dominatrix who would challenge him in ways that no Sub ever would. He'd been bored. Now, I wondered if that's all I'd really been to him – a different kind of challenge. Had he seen my inexperience as something new and fresh, something that would relieve the boredom? He'd told me that once he'd seen me, he hadn't wanted Juliette, and I believed that was the truth. What I'd never asked him was if being his lover had come from a different side of the same desire.

"Earth to Hanna."

Juliette snapped her fingers in front of my face, and I realized that we'd arrived at work. The building wasn't very big, but it didn't need to be. We didn't host events here. The reception area where Juliette and I had offices was small with barely enough room in the lobby for a few chairs, but the kitchen was easily four times that size, taking up the entire rest of the building. While Juliette did often handle first introductions to clients, she liked to involve herself in a little bit of everything, which was why she needed a business manager to make sure things weren't being overlooked in that department. I'd also taken on a lot of her assistant responsibilities since her last one had been arrested for kidnapping. Juliette hadn't decided yet if she wanted to hire a new one, and I couldn't really blame her. We were both bound to be wary of anyone new coming in.

"All of the details for Missie's brunch needs to be confirmed," Juliette said. "With Thanksgiving last week, I don't want to count on everyone making all of the notes they needed. It's too easy to get distracted when you're looking forward to time off."

I nodded my agreement as the two of us walked into the small but tastefully decorated lobby. Juliette didn't go in her office, however, but rather followed me into mine. I walked behind my desk and turned to see her standing on the other side.

"Are you going to be okay?" Juliette asked. Her expression was concerned, but there wasn't any pity in it, which I appreciated.

I nodded. "I need the distraction."

She came around the desk and put her hand on my arm. "If you want to talk..."

"I don't know what else to say," I admitted. "This wasn't some little squabble about not calling or arguing about who chose what we did last time. Even if it was only that one fight about the pregnancy test, it would've been bad enough, but the things he said yesterday..." My voice trailed off as my heart twisted painfully.

Juliette took my hand. "He'll realize how wrong he was, Hanna."

"Maybe." I squeezed her fingers and tried not to let my voice crack. "But I don't know what I'll do when that happens. *If* that happens."

"Do you still love him?"

My stomach twisted. "I'm furious with him, but I don't hate him. I can't." I swallowed hard. "I just don't know if I can be with him after seeing him this way. You warned me to stay away from him. I should've listened."

Juliette leaned back against my desk, her face somber. "I hoped I was wrong," she said. "I'd based it all on how he acted in the past, before he met you. I thought you'd changed him, and I still hope that's the case. If it's not, then he's the asshole I always thought he was."

Tears burned against my eyelids again. "I thought all of that was a front, that I saw the real man underneath, but what if I was wrong? What if this is who he really is? Cruel? Selfish?" I looked at her. "What if the man I love never really existed?"

She wrapped her arms around me, and I leaned into her. I hadn't meant to say it, hadn't intended to give voice to the thing I was most afraid of – that I'd fallen in love with an illusion – but I knew she wouldn't think badly of me for it.

I'd been sheltered as a child, but I'd never thought of myself as naive. Sure, the circumstances that brought Cross and me together were strange, but I hadn't wanted to consider that they'd given me a false read on the type of man Cross was.

"We'll get through this," Juliette said. "No matter what happens, you and I will get through it together."

It wasn't until then that I remembered that what I was going through was minor compared to what Juliette was dealing with. I was an adult dealing with a break-up. I'd survive. Juliette was dealing with so much more.

I took a step back. "Have you talked to either of those two men?"

I knew I didn't need to explain who I meant.

Juliette shook her head. "Not yet. I'm still not exactly sure what to tell them."

I rubbed the back of my hands across my eyes. "Looks like the two of us both have conversations coming that we don't want to have."

She chuckled. "We're a pair, aren't we?" She gave me a tight smile. "I'm glad you're here, Hanna. I wouldn't want to do this alone."

I returned the smile with one of my own. "Me too."

She straightened and nodded. "Right. Now, let's get

to work. Maybe we can distract ourselves from our guy problems."

I chuckled, feeling a bit more like myself than I had in days. This was what I needed. After Tucker and I broke up, I'd thrown myself into schoolwork and ended up graduating top of my class. If anything could divert me from Cross, this would be it.

I settled at my desk while Juliette went to her office. She'd be in and out all day, doing some paper work, some back in the kitchen. She often worked with the chefs on the menus, on making sure that all of the ingredients were included. I had calls to make, lists to check. It would've been a busy day even without all of this stuff going on with Cross and Juliette.

But it still wasn't enough.

I was scrolling through my checklist for the Nelson luncheon when I saw a familiar pair of names. Miranda Paulson and Jason Murphy. I didn't know their last names, but I was pretty sure they were the same people. The luncheon was to discuss fundraising for high school libraries, and I knew Miranda worked at one.

I'd always like the two of them. It was their performance that had given me my first taste of the BDSM world. But it wasn't only the erotic sensuality of the scene they'd performed but their relationship that I'd admired. They'd been a couple outside of the club, and from everything I'd seen, they were happy.

They were one of the reasons I thought it would be possible for Cross and me to do the same. I hadn't considered the fact that the reason the two of them worked so well together was because they wanted the same things. It appeared that Cross and I didn't.

Still, I couldn't stop thinking about how it felt to be in the club that night, the way it made me feel to watch

Miranda dominating Jason. The way I felt when Cross dominated me. Safe. Protected.

Loved.

I took a shuddering breath and tried to push the thoughts from my mind. I didn't want to think about him, or what he meant to me. Most of all, I didn't want to remember how he could make my body sing, how the thought of his touch turned me on. How just the memory of what it felt like with him inside me forced me to press my thighs together in an attempt to ease the ache.

Sex and love weren't enough, no matter how much I wished they were.

Chapter 12

Cross

Well, that was an idiotic move. Going to the club hadn't helped me get my mind off Hanna at all. In fact, all it made me do was think about all the things I wanted to do to her but couldn't. Which had only made me want to drink more.

So I had. I'd drank until I passed out on the couch.

I woke around noon with a raging headache, and a fucking erection hard enough to cut diamonds. I wrapped my hand around it without any real conscious thought, moaning as my fingers tightened.

It wasn't hard to imagine that it was a different hand moving over my cock. A smaller hand. I could almost hear the soft things she usually said when she was stroking me.

So hard, baby. Are you hard for me?

Look how big you are. Can barely get my fingers around you.

Can't wait to get you in my mouth. Taste you. Lick you. Suck you down until you're begging me to finish.

I'm so wet for you, baby. Can you feel how wet I am?

Hanna hadn't been much for dirty talk when we first met, but I'd encouraged her to say what she wanted, how she wanted it. I loved hearing her talk, loved knowing how she felt, how I made her feel.

My hand sped up, and my hips bucked up into my fist. Despite the pounding in my head, my balls tightened. I was close.

Most guys know how they like hand jobs by the time they reach their late teens because they've spent enough time with their hands on their dicks to know what they want. I'd always told women how to do things, including the first time Hanna had touched me, but more and more, she'd been doing her own thing, and I had to admit that she could do it better.

"Fuck," I muttered as I moved my hand faster. The friction was almost painful, but I embraced it. I deserved it.

I deserved a hell of a lot more...or less, I supposed, depending on how I looked at it. If I got what I deserved, I'd never have Hanna's hands on me again.

A vision of her flashed through my mind. Those beautiful eyes, darkened with pleasure. Lips slightly parted, ready for a kiss.

I groaned as I came, the hot liquid spilling over my hand and onto the sheets. It was a burst of pleasure, but it was a purely physical release. I felt no relief from the pain inside me. Nothing that made me feel any better. In fact...

I rolled out of bed, barely making it to the trash can before I lost whatever was in my stomach. The heaving made my head throb, the pressure so intense that I threw up again.

When I finally managed to get up without falling, I went to the bathroom and spent a half hour in the shower, trying to wash away the smell. It sobered me enough to be able to clean up my room as well. Unfortunately, even the handful of aspirin I took was barely taking the edge off the headache, which meant that every scent was heightened, every sight and sound magnified.

Once I finished cleaning up, I picked up my phone to make the call I was dreading. I cringed when I saw the twelve missed calls. This was not my day. My assistant picked up on the second ring.

"Mr. Phillips, I was getting worried."

I winced at the sound of his voice, but that was due more to my still throbbing temples than anything on his part. "I'm sorry, Abraham, the holiday got away from me. I won't be in today. If you could make apologies for me and reschedule things, I'll be in first thing tomorrow."

"Of course, sir."

We ended the call, and I stared at my screen before scrolling through the missed calls to clear things up. None of them were from Hanna. That wasn't a surprise. After the way I treated her, I didn't blame her for not texting or calling. I wouldn't want to talk to me either.

I tossed my phone down on the couch and looked around. I loved my home, loved the memories that came with staying in the place where I'd grown up. But right now, it felt far more empty than it ever had before. Hanna might not officially live with me, but I could feel her presence, see her everywhere.

We'd sat on this couch and talked, held each other while we watched movies. We'd made love here, sometimes soft and sweet, sometimes rough and fast. I could picture it with painful clarity. Her straddling my lap, skirt hitched up around her waist, breasts bared. Bending her over the arm of the couch, her panties hanging off one ankle.

The kitchen was just as bad. My mother and I had taken cooking classes together when I was twelve, and I'd always kept up my skills, especially after she was gone. It had always been my way of connecting with her. When I first brought Hanna here, I cooked for her. Then I started teaching her how to cook. We'd spent hours laughing and talking, tasting. I couldn't count how many times we'd gotten distracted, kissing, touching...more.

There wasn't a room in the entire house we hadn't christened. It wasn't even intentional. We just weren't able to keep our hands off each other. Sex had always been our way of reaching each other, comforting each other. Even when things had looked their bleakest, we could lose ourselves in each other.

I couldn't go back to the way things were before I met her. I wanted things the way they were with her before the disaster of last week.

That meant I'd have to get off my ass and do something about it. She made the first move by coming to see me yesterday, and I'd fucked that up. It was my turn to go to her.

I made myself another cup of coffee and drank it as I changed into jeans and a fitted charcoal gray shirt that I knew Hanna loved. Feeling almost completely sober and functional, I brushed my teeth, studied my reflection, and then headed out the door.

It wasn't until I arrived at the building Juliette and Hanna worked out of that my nerves made themselves known. I was taking a risk coming here, I knew. Juliette would be here. Other employees too. There was a chance they'd have clients, people who knew me. I could easily be humiliated in front of them. The smarter move would've been to wait until she was done, go to the apartment and talk to her there. Juliette would give us privacy.

But I couldn't wait that long. If I went home, I'd only spend the time pacing around, letting the anxiety build until I was ready to explode. I could go to the gym and try to burn off the excess energy there since my usual method of relieving stress wasn't an option, but I doubted I could concentrate. Going to work was out of the question. Even if my head was in it, I couldn't go in looking like this. I'd cleaned myself up, but it was still pretty clear how I'd spent the last couple days, and that wasn't something I wanted to show my employees.

No, I needed to get this taken care of right away. The risk of other people hearing us was worth it. I headed for the door before I could talk myself out of it.

"Hey, Elora." I greeted the receptionist with a smile. "Is Hanna busy?"

In her mid-forties, Elora DeBola had been with Juliette for two years and was probably the best receptionist I'd met. Courteous and polite, she had a way of telling people to go to hell that made them want to smile and thank her for it.

"She doesn't have any appointments," Elora said. "But I don't know if she's working on something. I'll ask."

"Don't." I managed to keep the smile on my face. "I'd like to surprise her."

Elora smiled at me, and I breathed a sigh of relief that Hanna hadn't told her to keep me out. That might have been because Hanna didn't think I'd show up here, but I wouldn't complain, not if it let me get in to see her.

I gave a light knock on the door so I wouldn't completely shock her, then opened it. She raised her head, and I watched as the color drained from her face. She looked exhausted, and even the make-up she was wearing couldn't hide the fact that she'd been crying.

In that moment, I hated myself. I loved her, and I'd hurt her like this.

I closed the door and walked around the desk, squatting so we were closer to eye level.

"You shouldn't be here." She finally found her voice.

"I know," I said, "but I have to be. I screwed up, Hanna."

She didn't say anything, but the expression on her face said that she agreed.

"I should never have left you in Ohio." I wanted to reach out, take her hand, but I had a feeling that she wouldn't want me to touch her. Not yet, anyway. "I should have stayed and talked to you, worked things out instead of letting them fester. I was an idiot."

"Yes," she said. "You were."

I counted it progress that she hadn't kicked me out yet, so I kept going. "I'm so sorry for the awful things I said. There's no excuse for any of it. I'm so sorry. Can you forgive me?"

Her eyes met mine, and I felt like she was searching for something. I didn't know what it was, but I hoped she'd find it. Unable to stop myself, I reached out and grasped one of her hands. It stayed limp for a moment as I curled my fingers around it, but then she squeezed back.

"I forgive you."

I moved to my knees and cupped the side of her face with my free hand. "Thank you." I brushed my lips across hers, grateful to finally touch her. "I hate fighting with you. These last few days have been miserable."

Her hand slid around the back of my neck, fingers playing with the short hair there. I ran both hands up her legs to her knees. I kept my eyes on hers as I pushed her legs apart and moved between them.

"I missed you," I said as I slid my hands higher,

90

pushing up her skirt as I went. "I missed you so much."

I took her mouth again, harder than before. All of the pent-up emotion, all of the desire and need came pouring out of me as I kissed her. My fingers dug into her thighs as my tongue plundered her mouth. I felt like I'd been given a reprieve. A dead man offered a second chance. I wasn't sure how close we'd come to breaking up, but I didn't even want to think about it. I had her back, and I planned to remind her how good we were together.

I kissed my way down her jaw, her neck, then lowered my head even as I slid my hands under her ass.

"Cross, not here."

I looked up at her even as I lifted her enough to remove her panties. "You know what to say if you really want me to stop."

Her eyes darkened as I tucked her underwear into my pants pocket, but she didn't say her safe word. My balls tightened. She wanted me as much as I wanted her.

I positioned her legs over my shoulders and gripped her hips tight to keep her in place. I wondered for a moment if the office was sound-proofed but then decided that I didn't care. If Hanna didn't want anyone else knowing what was going on, she'd have to keep herself quiet. Personally, I was hoping to make her scream.

The groan that escaped when I pressed my mouth against her made my cock harden. I held her in place as I slid my tongue between her folds. I loved going down on her, and not just because it meant that I'd eventually get to be inside her. I loved how wet she was, how she responded to my touch. Hell, I loved everything about this amazing body.

She buried a hand in my hair, tugging hard enough for it to hurt, but I didn't mind. Neither of us were masochists, but we both knew a little pain could add to the pleasure. Right now, the little jolts were making my erection press against my zipper.

Still, I stayed focused on my task. I was going to make her come at least once before I fucked her. I rubbed the flat of my tongue over her clit, then slid two fingers inside.

"Cross," she panted my name, and it was the most beautiful sound I'd ever heard. "Cross, please."

Her grip on my hair tightened. I curled my fingers, searching for that spot inside her. It didn't take me long to find it. Her entire body jerked as I pressed against the rough patched that made her go wild. I twisted my fingers even as I continued to tease her clit with my tongue and felt her body begin to tense. She was close.

"Please, Cross, please, please," she begged. She pulled my hair, moved her hips, trying to get whatever it was she needed to finally get off.

I looked up at her. "I've got you, baby."

I twisted my fingers, letting my knuckles rub against her g-spot. Her head fell back against her chair, and she came. I licked her sensitive skin, easing her down from her climax. When I pulled my fingers out, she whimpered. I licked them clean as I stood.

"Desk or chair?" I asked.

Hanna gave me a blank look.

I put my hands on the armrests of her chair and leaned over her. Damn. She was gorgeous most of the time, but this was how I thought she looked her best. Skin flushed with arousal, pupils wide, chest heaving. Limp and relaxed from an orgasm.

I pitched my voice low as I leaned close enough to smell her shampoo. "Do you want to fuck on the desk, or on the chair?"

"Probably not the best idea." She glanced at the door.

"Are you expecting someone?"

"Not until after lunch," she said.

I could see the conviction wavering, and I made my voice as stern as possible. "Desk or chair?" We might not have been in the club or in the playroom, but she knew what I sounded like when I was in charge.

"Desk."

I picked her up and turned, sitting her on the edge of her desk. She tilted her head up, the desire clear in her eyes, and I happily obliged her with a kiss. Even as our mouths moved together, my hands were busy undoing my jeans. She gasped into my mouth as I pushed inside her.

Fuck, she was so tight and hot. I wouldn't last long.

I nipped at her bottom lip, then moaned as her pussy tightened around me. Yeah, this was going to be quick.

"Touch yourself," I ordered as I began to move. "I'm going to come fast, and I want you there with me."

I felt her hand between us, fingers rubbing against us both as I thrust into her with short, hard strokes. I pressed my face against her neck, sucked skin into my mouth, worked it with my teeth even as she shuddered against me. I was going to leave a mark, one that would show everyone that she was mine.

Mine.

The word reverberated through me, and I groaned out her name as I came. A moment later, she followed me, her body stiffening once more. I wrapped my arms around her, holding her to me, needing to feel her body against mine, needing to know that she was mine.

"I love you," I murmured against her skin.

"I love you too."

And there we were. Relief swept through me. Everything was back to normal.

Chapter 13

Hanna

So, things were back to normal. After Cross left on Monday, he sent me a text asking to take me out to dinner. Then, yesterday, we met for lunch, and made plans for dinner tonight, with me staying over afterwards. It was like the whole thing over Thanksgiving never happened.

That should've made me happy. No more conflict, no wondering if the two of us were over. We were good together, able to enjoy sharing a meal...sharing a bed.

But I wasn't happy. Not really. I was glad that Cross had apologized, and that we weren't fighting anymore, but we hadn't talked about things. Not the things that caused the arguments. Cross hadn't said anything about why he'd freaked out so badly when he'd seen the pregnancy test, why he'd said the things he'd said. Saying that he was sorry and it'd all been blown out of proportion had been fine at the time, but I assumed we'd address the real issues at some point.

It didn't look like Cross planned on bringing it up, but if one of us didn't, then nothing would change. And someday, I needed things to move forward. Which meant I needed to know what had triggered the blow up.

It hadn't been Tucker because I was sure if Cross and I hadn't already been fighting, he never would've gone off about my ex. What we needed to talk about, I knew, was the whole baby / family freak out.

I was barely out of college, so it wasn't like I was asking for a ring and a baby right now, but I did want a family in the not-so-distant future. I wasn't like those girls back home whose entire life revolved around finding a husband and having children, but I also didn't want to be like Juliette, closing in on thirty and suddenly finding myself alone and pregnant. I refused to compromise on what I wanted in a man just so I could have a family, but I also wasn't going to waste my time on someone who didn't eventually want those things too.

I'd thought Cross and I were on the same page. I wasn't sure exactly why I thought that since we'd never actually talked about it. Maybe it was naive of me, but I'd just assumed that he'd wanted a family. He'd always sounded so lonely and wistful when he talked about his parents and not having siblings that I thought it meant he wanted something more than that.

But now I felt sure I was wrong.

The issue, however, was that I didn't know for certain. Which was why we needed to talk. And I was thinking sooner rather than later. I didn't want to drag it out if there would never be anything more between us. I loved him, but I wasn't going to spend the rest of my life as a girlfriend who sometimes spent nights at her rich boyfriend's place.

Better to end it now than in a few years when I would be too full of resentment and bitterness to have any fond memories at all.

At least, that's what I kept telling myself.

A lump formed in my throat and I fought the urge to

cry. There was no point in getting upset until I knew for sure what Cross was thinking.

Fortunately, I heard the door open, and I jumped at the distraction. Elora had gone to lunch, so I was covering the phones and greeting anyone who happened to come in. I hurried out into the lobby, a professional smile already on my face.

I had to admit, the man standing in front of me wasn't what I'd expected. Most people who came in to hire us were women, and the few men were generally older. This guy looked like he was about Cross's age, though not as expensively dressed. Hair the color of honey and an athletic body that his casual attire couldn't hide.

"Good morning," I said as I put out my hand. "I'm Hanna Breckenridge. How can I help you?"

"I'm Dalton Letlow." He smiled, but it didn't quite reach his dark blue-gray eyes.

Clearly, something was bothering him, but I doubted it was anything to do with food. "Are you looking to schedule an event?" I asked. "Or did you have questions regarding our menus? If you'd step into my office, we can discuss whatever it is that brought you here."

"Actually, I'm here to see Juliette." He ran his hand through his hair when he said her name, as if she was the reason he was distracted.

I wondered if that was a nervous gesture or if he was trying to make himself more presentable. If so, it really wasn't necessary. He looked good.

"She's in the back with our chefs," I said. "If you'll let me know what you're looking for, I might be able to assist you."

"She actually called me and left a voicemail saying she wanted to talk to me," Dalton said.

"I'll give her a call then." I motioned toward the pair of chairs that sat against the wall. "If you'd like to have a seat, I'm sure she'll be with you shortly."

Before I'd taken two steps toward my office, however, the door that led to the kitchen area opened and Juliette stepped out. I opened my mouth to tell her that she had a visitor, but when she looked up and saw Dalton, I knew I didn't need to say a word.

"Dalton? What are you doing here?"

That's when it hit me, and I realized that this was personal and not work related at all. I backed toward my office, hoping to avoid things becoming even more awkward, but I saw that I needn't have bothered. Neither one of them were even looking in my direction.

"You said you wanted to see me."

I'd never seen Juliette flustered, but it was clear she was right now. She pointed at her office.

"Let's talk somewhere private."

I was a little curious, but I knew if Juliette wanted to confirm who he was, she would. Meanwhile, I had work to do.

I went back into my office and pulled up the spreadsheet I needed to work on next. Things were ready for the Nelson luncheon, but I always liked to double-check. I methodically went through the list, letting the repetition turn into a rhythm that allowed me to focus on my work. With the completion of each task, I checked off things on the spreadsheet. When I finished with that, I emailed the completed file to Juliette letting her know that everything was on track for the luncheon.

I glanced out into the lobby to confirm that Elora was back, and then looked at Juliette's office. The door was closed, so I assumed she and Dalton were still talking. I went back to work and was in the middle of making up my final checklist for the Breashears brunch when Dalton walked past my office. His face was blank, eyes staring straight ahead. I heard Elora say something to him, but he didn't even pause to acknowledge her.

What the hell happened in there?

I got up and walked over to Juliette's office. The door was partly open, but I still knocked.

"It's me."

"Come in."

Juliette's voice was shaky, which didn't make me feel any better. When I pushed open the door and stepped into her office, I saw that she was sitting behind her desk, head in her hands. I closed the door behind me and sat down across from her.

"Are you okay?"

She raised her head, and a flare of anger went through me at whatever Dalton had said. Her face was pale, hands shaking as she clasped them together in front of her.

"What happened?" I reached across the desk and grabbed her hand. "What did that bastard do to you?"

Her laugh was a half-sob, and she took a deep, shuddering breath before meeting my eyes. "That's a great choice of words at the moment, Hanna."

I gave her a puzzled look.

"Remember how I told you that one of two men could've gotten me pregnant?" She didn't wait for me to answer before continuing, "I contacted the first guy, and he told me he'd had a vasectomy five years ago, so that ruled him out."

"Unless he was lying," I offered.

"I doubt that," she said. "He had it done after learning that he was a carrier for some genetic disease and never wanted to run the risk of passing it on to a kid, so he goes in every year to make sure nothing's grown back. Trust me, he wasn't lying."

I'd already put the pieces together, but I was going to let her say it. "And Dalton?"

She nodded. "He was guy number two, the one I'd picked up with the intention of having sex. We hadn't exchanged last names, and he hadn't hired me to dominate him, so it took me a couple days to track him down. I didn't realize he'd come here."

Her voice was starting to crack, so I gave her hand a squeeze. "It's okay."

The words sounded weak, some sort of rote platitude given to people out of obligation, but I couldn't think of anything else to say.

"I'd always prided myself on how careful I am," she said. "On the pill and using condoms. Hell, most of the time, I even insist on condoms for oral sex."

She leaned back in her chair, releasing my hand. She'd talked a bit about how the odds of this happening had been so low she'd never thought it possible, but I could tell that, now, the reality of it all had hit her.

"He was quite the gentleman about it. He didn't blame me," she murmured. "Dalton, I mean. I told him about the antibiotics and how we must've had a faulty condom, and he didn't act like it was my fault at all. He didn't even ask if I was sure he was the father."

"What did he say?" I asked.

"That he needed time to process and think," she said. "I told him I completely understood. I mean, I've had almost a week to come to terms with it. I couldn't expect him to immediately know what he wants. He said he'd call me in a couple days, and we'd set up a time to talk in more detail."

"He seems nice enough," I offered.

Juliette shrugged. "I barely know him well enough to be able to agree with that. I mean, I know he's a Sub, and how he likes sex, but I don't know his middle name or his birthday." She shook her head. "I don't know what to do, Hanna. I mean, can you imagine the looks on our parents' faces if they find out I got knocked up by some one-night stand?"

I got up and walked around the desk. I leaned down and wrapped my arms around her. She leaned into me as I kissed the top of her head. "It'll all work out, Juliette. You'll see. And whatever you decide to do, I'm with you. You won't go through this alone."

"Thanks." She put her arms around my waist. "I'm so glad you moved out here."

"Me, too."

I was, truly, but I also was a bit relieved that Juliette couldn't see my face and know that, even though I was grateful to be here to help her, a part of me wondered how things would've been different if I'd stayed at home, if I'd never met Cross. I loved my sister, and I loved Cross, but I couldn't help thinking that my life might've been a lot easier if I'd just listened to my parents and stayed in Zanesville.

Chapter 14

Cross

After last week, I'd been worried that everything was going to fall apart, but since I'd talked to Hanna on Monday, things had gone back to normal. We'd talked and texted just like always. We had dinner together, had lunch, made love. It was all perfect.

I'd even been able to concentrate at work all week, which was a good thing since my absence on Monday had left me with a completely packed schedule. I had meetings to run and business deals to look over, people to meet with. And my time with Hanna was exactly what it should have been – a much needed distraction with my wonderful girlfriend.

I leaned back in my seat. Today's schedule was easier than earlier in the week, which meant I didn't have anyone coming in until after lunch. I had a couple phone calls to return, but not much else for the next hour. Usually, I'd spend the time looking over other business possibilities, considering various charities to support, perhaps even new ones to found.

At the moment, however, I preferred to use the time to think about how well things had gone over the last couple days. The dinner we'd made side by side. One of the reasons I'd enjoyed cooking lessons with my mother had been that we'd spent time together, just the two of us. With Hanna, I appreciated not only the opportunity for us to do something together, but I liked teaching her things, and not only in the bedroom.

There was also the fact that, even in a kitchen as large as mine, cooking put us in close proximity to each other. One of the things I loved to do was build anticipation. The caress of a shoulder, the brush of a hip. It was a part of a relationship that I hadn't been able to take advantage of before. Usually, the only way I got to work on anticipation was once the clothes were off, and sex was coming up fairly soon. This was different.

Well, sort of. I'd only been able to deal with not having my hands on bare skin for so long before I'd put Hanna on the counter and fucked her while our food was cooking. I could still hear her calling out my name as she came, feel her tightening around me. It'd made dinner so much more interesting knowing that her panties were soaked with my cum. As soon as we'd finished eating, I'd had her take them off and straddle my lap.

I reached down to adjust myself. Thinking about sex with Hanna was a sure-fire way to spend the rest of the day with a hard-on. Not exactly the condition I wanted to be in during my afternoon meetings. At least one of the guys would've thought it was funny, but I didn't want to be unprofessional.

So I made myself think about other things. Facts and figures from sales reports. Blueprints for buildings. Anything that was boring and didn't automatically make me think of Hanna or sex.

Once I'd calmed my libido, I reached for my keyboard, ready to get some work done. I hadn't gotten very far when Abraham buzzed me.

"Mr. Phillips, there's a young woman here to see you."

I frowned. I didn't have any young women on my schedule for the day, and Abraham knew Hanna so he would've just said her name.

"She says it's important that she speak to you, sir," Abraham continued. "Should I schedule her an appointment for next week?"

I looked at my computer and the list of details I had to go over, then thought about how nice a distraction would be. I leaned over and pressed the intercom button. "Send her in."

The woman who walked in looked like she was a little younger than me but not quite as young as Hanna. She was pretty, but I was willing to wager that her curves drew more attention than her face. They were superb. Judging by the way she walked, she knew it too. Shoulder-length dark blonde hair and, as she drew closer, I noticed dark blue eyes.

I stood and held out a hand. "Good morning, Miss...?"

"Carver," she said. Her voice was low and husky. "Taliyah Carver."

She shook my hand, then dropped into the seat across from me. She crossed one leg over the other and gave me an expectant look. I sat down and took a moment to study her. I'd never seen her before, I was sure of that, but she looked like she knew me. Then again, that wasn't surprising. A lot of strangers knew me. I wasn't the kind of celebrity people thought of when they thought of Hollywood, but anyone interested in the old money families who'd helped found this area could easily learn about me.

"How can I help you, Miss Carver?" I asked, breaking the silence.

"I have a story to tell you, Mr. Phillips," she said with a smile.

Not what I was expecting, but I had to admit, it piqued my curiosity, and that hadn't happened in a long time. If I was honest about it, it was boredom that had first made me want to approach Juliette in the first place. Of course, it wasn't Juliette I'd met, but rather Hanna, and I was grateful for it, but it'd been a while since anything had surprised me.

"Go ahead."

She gave me another one of those little smiles. "In Nashville, Tennessee, almost thirty years ago, there was a singer by the name of Layla. She came from a poor family but was determined to make something of herself. No one believed in her, no one encouraged her, but she worked hard, sang wherever she could, whenever she could."

I wasn't entirely sure where she was going with this, but I wouldn't cut her off just yet. Something in my gut told me to hear her out.

"One day, she was singing in this little hole-in-the-wall club, the kind of place that people went to have private conversations, and a man catches her eye. He's handsome, and clearly far too rich for this place. She knows the man he's sitting with. He's the sort of talent scout who takes advantage of women, getting them to have sex with him for promises of movie and television roles. He'd been after her for years."

I knew the type, unfortunately, but I'd done my best to make sure I never dealt with those sorts of people.

"Layla, of course, knew to avoid the talent scout, but when the other man came to see her, she couldn't resist.

He made her promises that she believed but didn't follow through on. He wasn't the same as the talent scout, selling sex, but he did something so much worse. He told her that he loved her, that he wanted to marry her. But he was already married. Had a child, in fact. When she found out, she left him, vowing never to see him again. It wasn't until several weeks later that she realized she would always have a part of him with her. She was pregnant."

I tried not to scowl. I'd been curious, but now I was just annoyed. I hoped she'd get to the point. And not the point I had a feeling she was heading to.

"The requisite number of months later, and I was born." She smiled at me.

"That's a nice story," I said. "But I'm not quite sure why you're telling me."

"Aren't you?" She uncrossed her legs and leaned forward, her eyes glinting. "Your father never told you about my mother, or me, did he?"

The words didn't make sense. Couldn't make sense. "My father?" I was proud of myself for sounding nonchalant.

"Come now, Cross. Let's not play around like this." She leaned back again and pulled a cigarette from her purse.

"You can't smoke in here," I said firmly. "And I'd appreciate if you'd stop with the storytelling and speak plainly, Miss Carver."

"All right," she said. "You want me to speak plainly? How's this for plain: your father fucked my mother under false pretenses, and then ignored me, both when he was alive and even after he died." She smiled, twirling the cigarette between her fingers. "I'm your half-sister."

Chapter 15

Hanna

I got off later than I'd expected, so Cross was already at his house when I got there. We'd planned on making dinner together, so I went to the kitchen first. On the counter was a note.

In the shower, babe. Go ahead and get started without me.

I flushed even though the note was totally innocent. Well, maybe not totally. It would be like Cross to have written about being in the shower because he wanted me thinking about him being naked and wet.

My entire body throbbed at the image of him standing under the shower head, letting the water trickle down over those broad shoulders, that firm torso, down...down...down...

"Fuck me," I muttered. He was damn lucky I was hungry because, otherwise, I would've *really* started without him.

Even now, my fingers itched to be under my skirt, under my panties, stroking myself, feeling my slick arousal, bringing myself to the edge of orgasm...then stopping just before I got there because I knew Cross would punish me if I came without him. A part of me

109

almost wanted to do it, wanted him to punish me. As much as I enjoyed the gentle side of Cross, the tender love making we sometimes experienced, another part of me craved the more primal side of things.

We talked about it when he first introduced me into the BDSM world, and I'd understood it, even though I couldn't explain it. There was something inside me that wanted to be claimed, that wanted to feel him taking me hard and rough, as if his desire was too much for something slow.

No, not wanted. Needed. I needed it.

The intensity of the feeling still took me off-guard sometimes, how much I needed him. I could still function on my own, could still stand on my own two feet, but I knew, now that I'd opened myself up to this world, there would always be a part of me that needed what he gave me.

And that scared me, thinking about losing him when I knew how much he meant to me.

I pushed the speculations aside and walked over to the refrigerator. We'd planned on making a stir-fry, so I pulled out the vegetables we'd need. I'd finished slicing the tomatoes and peppers and was washing off my hands when I heard him behind me. I turned, mouth open to tell him what I'd done...and froze.

Damn.

He had a towel wrapped around his waist, but that was it. His chest glistened with the moisture he hadn't wiped away, and his hair was still wet enough to drip onto his shoulders. As my eyes trailed down over his chest to that thin line of hair, I forgot that I was hungry for anything other than him.

Without a word, he closed the distance between us and captured my mouth in a scorching kiss. His hands slid down my back to cup my ass, and then he was lifting me. The towel fell away as I wrapped my legs around his waist. The thought of how he must look, muscles flexing as he walked with us, made me moan into his mouth. I loved his body, the feel of it, the way it looked.

When my back was against the wall, Cross moved one hand between us. I felt my panties tear more than I heard them, but I couldn't manage the words to scold him. I'd probably care about the underwear tomorrow, but right now, I only cared about him.

I cried out as he shoved inside me. I was wet, but there'd been no foreplay, and he stretched me too fast, too much. He wrapped his hand in my hair, yanking my head to the side as he fucked me. His kisses on my throat were rough, nips with his teeth then soothed with his tongue. I squeezed my eyes closed and hung on, unable to do anything else but try to deal with the overwhelming sensations coursing through me.

When I came, it crashed over me without any warning. Cross swore as my body tightened around him, then he was pulling out, sending another ripple of pleasure through me as he rubbed against my g-spot on his way. I barely registered that we were moving again, and then I was bent over the table, my legs trembling as they struggled to hold me.

He shoved my skirt up around my waist, baring my shredded panties and the flesh they revealed. The first time his hand came down on my ass, I yelped, more from surprise than the sting. Three more cracks, two on either cheek and I was dripping. I propped myself up on my elbows as Cross slid his hands up my ribcage and then around to move underneath my shirt. His cock pressed against my hip, hot and hard, and I pushed back against him, wanting him inside me again.

"Be a good girl," he whispered in my ear as he shoved my bra up over my breasts. "I'm not feeling very gentle at the moment."

His words shouldn't have sparked a flame of desire in me, but they did.

"What if I don't want to be good?" I asked, looking over my shoulder to meet his eyes.

The heat that flared there made my mouth go dry. He squeezed my breasts hard enough to hurt, and I whimpered but didn't protest. His fingers found my nipples, rolling and pinching until they were throbbing in time with my pussy.

He used his knee to nudge my legs apart as he straightened, and then his cock was pressing against me. My eyelids fluttered as he slid himself deep inside. It was easier than the prior time, but still enough to make us both groan.

"I'm going to fuck you now." He leaned over me and pushed his thumb into my mouth. "And you're going to come with my thumb in your ass."

I scraped my teeth over the pad of his thumb, then worked my tongue around it, knowing that this was probably all of the lubrication I would get.

"Then, after dinner, we'll spend some time in the playroom."

I shivered and heard him curse as the movement caused me to tighten around him. Then his thumb was gone, and he was driving into me with enough force to make me see stars. Over and over, he filled me, the head of his cock rubbing against my g-spot until the friction was almost painful. When he started to work his thumb into my ass, I came again. My arms gave out and my breasts pressed against the cool tabletop. His thumb twisted even as he moved faster. Just when it started to become more than I could take, he went over the edge, his cock emptying inside me. His hips rocked against me, coaxing out the last drop of pleasure for both of us before pulling out. I gasped at the sudden loss, then flushed as his semen trickled down my thigh.

Cross smacked my still exposed ass and gave me a self-satisfied grin. "Why don't you go get cleaned up while I finish making dinner?"

And then he was walking back to the kitchen, whistling as he went.

I stayed there for a moment, still regaining my breath, and then straightened. I pulled my skirt down and adjusted my bra even though I planned to change out of them both. Cross might not have any qualms about walking around naked, but I wasn't quite that comfortable.

I went to the bathroom off the master bedroom and stripped out of my clothes. I scowled at my torn panties and tossed them in the trash. I didn't bother with a shower, settling instead for a quick clean-up and then slipped on the robe I kept here. If we were going to the playroom after we ate, there really wasn't a point in a shower or clothes. I wouldn't be surprised if Cross ate naked just so he'd have less to take off later.

When I stepped back into the kitchen, however, he was wearing a pair of sweatpants that he must've grabbed when I was in the bathroom. He looked over his shoulder at me and smiled.

"Just finishing up."

A few minutes later, we settled at the table with our plates and began to eat.

"How'd the Nelson thing go?" Cross asked. "You guys weren't working it, right? Just bringing in the food."

I nodded. "It went off without a hitch, which was

good because Juliette's already freaking out about the brunch tomorrow."

"Why?" he asked. "She's worked with Missie Breashears before. I thought they got along well."

"They do," I said. "But Juliette heard that there's supposed to be some bigwigs there, and she wants to make a good impression. She's decided that she wants to stop supplementing her income from being a dominatrix."

"Yeah, that might be a bit hard to keep up once she starts showing," Cross said as he reached for his glass of wine.

"Is it dangerous?" I asked, both curious and concerned. "I mean, I know it's safe to have sex for most of the duration of a pregnancy, but I don't know about any of this other stuff."

"I'm not sure." He shrugged. "I was thinking more along the lines of no one wanting to be dominated by a pregnant lady."

I stared at him, a sick feeling forming in my stomach. Fortunately, he was looking down at his plate, and I managed to hide my expression by the time he looked up. I pushed the food around on my plate, suddenly not very hungry.

Was that it? Was that the real reason the pregnancy test had freaked him out? Why he said all that shit when he'd been drunk? I'd assumed a fear of commitment was the issue, or even that he was simply comfortable where we were and had no desire to change things.

I'd never once imagined that the reason he might not want to get married or have kids was something so fucking selfish and superficial as the way my appearance would change if I became pregnant. It wasn't like I expected any man to get turned on by a random pregnant woman, but I'd always assumed that a decent man would still want the partner who was carrying his child.

Then again, that was going with the assumption that Cross was a decent man. The events of the last couple weeks had begun to make me think differently.

When he said he loved me, I truly believed that was unconditional, that even if something happened to me, he'd still want to be at my side. I'd never been one of those women who feared that if they gained weight, started looking old, were diagnosed with some sort of disease, that their partner would leave them.

Even when Tucker had broken up with me, I'd never thought it was because of how I looked or anything like that. I'd completely understood it, even if it had hurt. He hadn't had the self-control needed to maintain a long-distance relationship, but that hadn't been because of me. He wouldn't have been able to make it with anyone that way.

As I sat across from Cross now, I was forced to admit how little I truly knew about him, and how much had just been things I'd assumed. I'd thought they were conclusions drawn from facts I'd observed, but now I could see that most had been because of what I wanted to be true.

At first, I'd worried that our relationship had taken off too quickly, that the circumstances under which we'd gotten together had prevented us from progressing naturally. But things had gone so well that I'd decided Cross and I were so perfect for each other that there was no point in us trying to take things slow.

I just hadn't stopped to think that part of what usually came as part of a normal relationship's progression was talking about things like this, about marriage and kids. Now, I saw the reality of who Cross was, and I didn't know if I could be with a man like that.

"I'm not feeling well," I blurted out, then pushed back my chair and stood. "I think I'll get dressed and go home."

"Hanna?"

I heard Cross stand as he said my name, but I was already heading back toward the bedroom. I couldn't look at him.

"Babe, are you okay? Do you need me to take you to the hospital?" He followed me.

"No." I shook my head as I pulled out the first pair of pants and shirt I found.

"Was I too rough?"

His voice was so gentle, so caring, that I wanted to give in, to let him hold me and comfort me. But I couldn't, because that would lead to sex, and the way I was feeling right now, I didn't want to try to make that connection. Not that he'd ever force me, but when his hands were on me, I couldn't think straight.

"No," I said again. "I'm just not feeling well, and with the brunch tomorrow, I can't afford to get sick."

"At least let me call you a car to take you home," he offered.

"I can make it on my own." I brushed by him without looking up. "I'll text you when I get there so you won't worry."

I felt his eyes on me as I left, but he didn't try to stop me, didn't come after me to insist on going with me. It was just like what happened before. He had no clue what he said wrong. Granted, this last comment hadn't sparked an argument, so I couldn't really expect him to get it, but considering how he'd behaved before, I had no reason to think he'd even think that what he said was hurtful.

Cross lived in his own little world. If things didn't affect him, they didn't matter. I didn't know why I hadn't seen it before, but it made me realize that I needed to rethink being a part of his world.

A part of me wished I'd never invited him back to Ohio for Thanksgiving, but I knew that it was better to find out now instead of wasting too much time on someone who didn't share the same values as I did.

I'd focus on the brunch, and then talk to Cross when he called tomorrow evening to discuss plans for the rest of the weekend. We'd hash things out between us, and then I could start looking at where I wanted to go in the future.

Chapter 16

Hanna

I was pretty sure I looked like shit, but Juliette was nice enough not to mention it. I tried to cover the dark circles under my eyes, but they were still visible to anyone who cared enough to notice. I made sure to dress pristinely and to actually style my usually crazy curls, hoping that would take the attention from how tired I clearly was. Or, if anyone noticed, they'd assume I'd been working too hard.

Juliette knew the truth, though not all of it. I wasn't about to tell her what Cross had said about a pregnant dominatrix. I'd kept his comments vague, saying that he made a couple comments that had made me wonder if I needed to reconsider our relationship. Since she'd already known about the arguments we'd had recently, a further detailed explanation hadn't been needed.

"Juliette!" Missie Breashears came toward us, arms open. She gave my sister two of those air kisses that I always thought only happened in the movies, and then turned to me. "Hanna, darling."

She leaned forward, and I let her greet me the same

way. In her mid-fifties, Missie barely looked a day over forty-five, and unlike many women who used surgeries and shots that ended up making them look like plastic, Missie's youthful appearance was all natural. Her sepia brown curls were probably dyed but done so well that it was impossible to tell. The clothes she wore were expensively tailored, but not ostentatious like a lot of the people around here who thought they had to prove they had money.

"Everything looks wonderful," Missie said. "The guests will probably be arriving shortly. Is there anything you need from me?"

Juliette shook her head. "Everything's right on schedule."

"Excellent." Missie headed back into the main room.

I glanced at Juliette. "You do remember that half of our wait staff is running late thanks to an accident downtown, right?"

She nodded. "Already have that covered."

I raised an eyebrow. "You do?"

"If they're not here on time, you and I will help cover the appetizers and drinks until they get here."

I frowned. I hadn't liked playing hostess at the last event we'd done for Missie, and this would be direct interaction with hundreds of people. Not exactly my favorite thing to do. I was fine with people if I had a specific purpose for talking to them, or if I was mingling for a specific reason. This sort of thing, however, tended to make me a little nervous.

And when I was nervous, I sometimes said things that I wouldn't have said otherwise.

"Have you talked to Dalton again?"

Juliette turned and gave me a hard look. "Not the time or place, Hanna." Her voice was flat. "We don't need

120

to discuss personal matters right now. We have work to do."

"You're right," I said. "Sorry."

And she was right. Thinking about the crazy turns my own life had taken recently had made me think about the issues she was dealing with, but I shouldn't have brought them up here.

"I need to focus on work right now," she said. "We both do."

I nodded. We couldn't afford to get distracted, not with so much riding on this brunch. Even as I thought it, I realized that was why she wanted us to help serve. We could play it off as wanting to make sure the guests had everything they needed, assuring them that we were handling everything, but Juliette wanted it as much to make connections with new people.

Even if she wasn't admitting it, she was thinking about the baby. She said she hadn't made up her mind what she wanted to do, and I was sure if I asked her, she would've said she was preparing for all contingencies, or that she'd always intended to pull back from her dominatrix role. While that may have been partially true, I knew that she never would've done any of this if she wasn't at least seriously considering keeping the baby.

We'd never really talked about it, I realized. We'd discussed sex and relationships of that nature, but never whether or not she wanted a family. It wasn't like she refused to discuss the subject, but rather more like it'd never been brought up. Our parents had always harped on getting married and having kids, and I was sure that Juliette had gotten it worse than me since she was the oldest, so it really wasn't surprising that she didn't want to talk about it.

She glanced at her watch. "I'll go check the progress

on the appetizer trays. Can you call Patrick and see if they're still stuck in traffic?"

I nodded and went to retrieve my phone from my purse. After a brief conversation, I had an answer that Juliette wouldn't like. I headed back to the main preparation area where Juliette was shifting plates around on a tray to accommodate additional ones.

"This pattern lets you get almost half a dozen more plates onto each tray," she explained. "You just have to remember to balance things out as you remove the plates. Don't take all from the inside, and shift your fingers to compensate for the change in weight as you remove each plate."

She glanced up as I walked in, and I could see the frustration in her eyes. She wasn't taking it out on the poor server, but she was annoyed. Patrick was the head of the wait staff, and he was usually the one who made sure all of the trays were loaded correctly. He also had three of our most experienced servers with him, which meant we had to explain things that would normally just be taken care of.

"Did you talk to Patrick?"

I nodded as I moved to her side. I kept my voice down as I repeated what he'd told me. "The police were in the middle of setting up a detour when a water main burst. They're moving, but they have to go out and around. It'll be at least a half hour before they get here."

"In time for clean up and dessert, but not here to deliver main courses." Juliette sighed and closed her eyes for a moment.

I didn't say anything. She was thinking.

She opened her eyes again. "I need the server flow chart you made."

I opened the binder where I kept track of all the

information needed to allow things to go smoothly. Juliette had one too. We each had our own files, as well as copies of the other's work to serve as back-ups as needed. I flipped to the correct section and pulled out the paper. I handed it to her and then joined her in studying it.

For an event of this size, to ensure that no one was missed and that there weren't any accidents involving servers running into each other, we had a flow chart that showed where each server was working, as well as the path they were supposed to take. With four of them now absent, it had to be completely reworked.

"All right," she said as she pulled a pen from her pocket. "Here's what we're going to do."

I watched as she redrew the lines to compensate for the changes, then frowned when I saw the strange path she'd made for the two of us. I'd started making these charts myself recently, but I'd watched Juliette do it dozens of times first, listened to her explain how each path was specifically designed to make the best use of space, to make sure people's food wasn't the wrong temperature. This, however, didn't follow those guidelines.

"What are you doing?" I asked.

At least she didn't try to insult my intelligence by acting like she didn't know what I was talking about.

"I got the final seating chart from Missie," she said. "If we're going to be serving, I want to take advantage of it and make sure it gives me the chance to introduce myself to the people I want to know."

"Then why is mine so weird?" I asked.

She grinned at me. "I figured I'd take the most important people, but with you here, you could cover the people of secondary importance."

I chuckled. Leave it to Juliette to figure out how to

use something most caterers would consider a disaster as a way to boost her business. And to rate all of the guests in such a way that she could decide who she wanted to talk to, and who it was better to relegate to me.

These were one of those times where I could see how staying in Zanesville would've been a total waste of her talents. RJ was being groomed to take over the shop once our parents retired, and even if Juliette had taken over the management part of things, it always would've been RJ's business. I might've been okay with that. I didn't mind not being the owner of the business, but Juliette would've chaffed under anyone else's authority, especially our brother's. I loved the guy, but he could be insanely bossy. It drove me nuts, but it would've been worse for Juliette since she was older.

"Is there anything specific you want me to say to any of them?" I asked.

"Introduce yourself, tell them you're the business manager, let them know that if there's anything you or I can do to help them, to just let us know." Juliette took the altered chart and tacked it up on the board she'd brought with her. It covered the chart that was already on there. "Attention!" She raised her voice so that everyone could hear her. "Patrick and the others are running late, so we need to change things around a bit. Here's how we'll do it until they get here. Hanna and I will take these two routes, everyone else, here's how the others are broken up."

The other servers moved closer so that they could see how things had changed. They didn't even blink an eye at hearing that Juliette and I were going to help. I didn't know any of them well, but they were good people, hard workers.

"Everyone memorize the new routes, and we'll be

back as soon as Mrs. Breashears is ready for us."

Juliette motioned for me to follow her. We stood off to the side, watching as people came in.

"That's Harvey Dallas. He'll be at one of your tables, but not because I don't already know him." She gestured toward a short, stocky man who was just coming in. "Make a point of telling him that you're dating Cross."

"Just him?" My stomach squirmed at the mention of the man I loved.

She shrugged. "Might need to tell some other people, but him for certain. He's seen me at the clubs sometimes and has a little thing for me. As soon as he sees you, he'll know we're related. If you drop Cross's name, he'll leave you alone."

"Thanks for the warning." The words came out automatically, but I was having a hard time listening, focusing on anything except the name that she said.

Cross.

I didn't want to think about Cross right now. I needed to concentrate on work, on doing what Juliette needed me to do. Right now, I didn't know if Cross would ever be my family, but Juliette already was and always would be. She and work were my priority right now.

Cross would have to wait.

Chapter 17

Cross

Hanna's name flashed across my screen for the second time, and for the second time, I let it go to voicemail. She called a couple hours ago to let me know that she'd finished up at the brunch. I was supposed to have called her back so we could talk about plans for this weekend, if she was coming over tonight or tomorrow.

Except I hadn't called her back that first time, and I didn't intend to call her back this time. Something was wrong, and I didn't know how to address it. Hell, I didn't even know what it was. Everything had been great last night. We'd had hot, fantastic sex, and dinner had been delicious. We'd planned on spending several quality hours in the playroom. Then, all of a sudden, without any warning, she said she wasn't feeling good and left.

I had no reason to doubt her, but as soon as she'd gone to get dressed, my stomach had twisted itself into knots. She hadn't stopped to talk to me, and by the time she was out the door, I'd had a bad feeling that things had gone wrong for some reason, though for the life of me, I couldn't figure out how.

When I woke up this morning – which wasn't really accurate since I hadn't exactly slept – I decided to keep myself busy until I decided what I wanted to do. It seemed like no matter how hard I tried to keep the two of us on track recently, things just kept getting worse.

And it was starting to piss me off.

It wasn't like I didn't have anything else going on in my life at the moment. I leaned back in my chair and ran my hand through my hair for what seemed like the millionth time today.

Taliyah Carver.

What was it with the fucking women in my life right now? First Hanna wanting me to meet her family, and that stirring up a whole shit storm, then some stranger coming in and telling me that she was my sister.

Half-sister, I clarified.

But that didn't make it any better. In a way, it was worse. Okay, not in a way. In every way.

Her whole story had been going round and round in my head from the moment she'd finished telling it. I'd spent every hour since then trying to distract myself, trying to keep my mind from going back to what she'd said and the implications of what that meant. But after Hanna left last night, my only choices regarding what I was going to brood about were Hanna or Taliyah, neither of which were really appealing. The problem was, they were the only two things vying for my attention.

This morning, I decided that Taliyah was the lesser of two evils. At least with her, I had a better idea of what I needed to deal with.

The first of which was the most obvious one.

If what she said was true, if she was indeed my half-sister, no matter how much truth there was to her story, it still meant that my father had slept with someone else while he was married to my mother.

I wasn't naive enough to think that my parents had

been perfect. I was young when they died, but not a child. I didn't idealize or romanticize who they'd been. I knew they both had their faults, their weaknesses. I just never imagined that either of my parents had had affairs.

And I sure as hell hadn't imagined that either of them had a child somewhere out there. A child they'd ignored and abandoned.

I knew that there was a possibility she was lying. People in positions of power or with money often had people claiming to be relatives. Fortunately, the progression of science had done a lot to help keep people in my position from being taken advantage of. All I had to do was ask for a DNA sample, and I'd know the truth.

However, because most people were smart enough to know that, only those who were extremely confident in their manipulative ability were able to fake test results...or were flat-out crazy.

I had a bad feeling Taliyah wasn't any of those things. That she was telling the truth, and we shared the same father.

So I decided that I needed to get my head wrapped around that before anything else. If, for some reason, the test results came back negative – which I supposed could still happen if Taliyah's mother had lied to her – I'd be okay, but I'd also be prepared if it was the truth.

Except I wasn't entirely sure how to process it. How to accept that I actually had a sister when I always thought I was an only child, that I had no family. A sister only three years younger than me. The way she'd talked, it sounded like she'd always known who her father was and that she'd assumed that he'd known about her, but hadn't wanted to be part of her life.

I couldn't see how that would be possible though. Even if my father hadn't wanted my mother to know that he'd had an affair, I couldn't see my father completely writing off a child of his. He might not have been a faithful husband, but he'd been a great father.

I spent the morning searching through the boxes of my parents' things that I kept in the house, but I hadn't found anything that hinted at Taliyah's existence. It was possible I'd gotten rid of something a few years ago when I'd cleaned out most of Mom and Dad's stuff, but there was nothing I could do about that.

I couldn't ask my parents' friends because there hadn't been anyone they were especially close to. Not close enough to talk about something like that.

Except there was someone Dad would've confided in, if only for legal reasons. I knew my father, and if he'd known about Taliyah, he would've made legal provisions for her.

I picked up my phone, but not to call Hanna back. Scott Vernon had been our family lawyer since I was a kid, had come to more than one of the holiday parties my parents had thrown. He'd handled their estate, helped me set up my own will after they were gone so that, if something happened to me, there'd be no doubt over where my assets would go.

Which meant I had his home number.

It was still early evening, so I tapped his contact information and let the phone ring.

Scott answered on the third. "Cross Phillips. How're you doing?"

"I'm doing well, Scott. How're you?"

"Good, good. Can't complain." The noise in the background faded.

"Did I catch you at a bad time?" I asked. I wanted answers, but I wasn't going to be rude about it.

"Not at all," he said. "My wife's book club is over.

I'm actually glad for a chance to get out of there. Now, what can I do for you?"

I hadn't thought that far ahead. I closed my eyes. "I don't know of any other way to say this, but to just come out and say it."

"This sounds serious," Scott said, his voice sobering.

"You were responsible for all of my father's legal affairs," I said.

"Yes."

"Did he ever ask for you to include any...private provisions?"

"'Private provisions'?" he echoed. "Cross, what is it you suspect your father of needing to keep private?"

"Did he have another child?" I blurted out the question. "I mean, was there anything he had you set up for another woman or for another child?"

There was a long silence before he spoke again. "Is there a reason for this line of questioning?"

He was all business now.

"Does that mean you do know something?" An icy hand gripped my heart. If Scott had known all this time that I had a sister...

"Your father wasn't a perfect man," he said slowly. "As I'm sure you know. He loved you and your mother very much and didn't let any of his errors in judgement influence how he felt about you."

I felt sick. "So you know that he had affairs." I made it a statement rather than a question.

Another pause. "I know that he had at least two. And you should know that he instructed me to be honest with you if you ever asked."

I took a slow breath. "Did he have money set aside for those women?"

"No. And I wouldn't have even called them

mistresses. Both were one-night stands. A weekend at the most."

That fit with what Taliyah had told me. Now came the question I needed answered the most. "Did he have any other children?"

"Of course not!" Scott sounded insulted that I even asked, and that, more than anything, convinced me that he was telling the truth. "Your father would never have kept that from you."

"Not even to keep Mom from finding out about his affairs?"

Another beat of silence. "Your parents told each other everything, Cross, including their indiscretions...on both parts."

"So, my mom..."

"I considered your parents my friends," Scott said. "So I might've known a little more about their personal lives than I do about my other clients. Their marriage was more solid than most people's, and they always said that was because they were honest about everything."

"Did they—" I almost couldn't make myself say it. "Did they have an open marriage?"

"Not exactly. More like an agreement that they wouldn't fight about sleeping with someone once or twice, but that there'd be no long-term affairs, no divorcing to be with someone else."

Which meant my father had either broken that agreement, lied to Taliyah's mother, or Taliyah's mother had lied to her. Any of them were possible.

"Not even if a kid was involved?"

"I can't say anything one hundred percent," he admitted. "But I'd be willing to bet everything I have that if your father had another kid, he would've provided for him."

"Okay." I closed my eyes. "Thanks, Scott. I appreciate it."

"Want to tell me what's going on?"

"Not really," I admitted. "But if it turns out to be something, I'll come to you first."

"Make sure you do," he said. "Have a good night, kid."

I ended the call and tossed my phone down on the seat next to me. So, now I had confirmation that my father had indeed had an affair. More than one. And that my mother had too, but that had nothing to do with Taliyah.

Someone was lying, but I still didn't know exactly who yet.

I leaned forward and opened my laptop. First thing Monday, I'd call Mars Roster, a private investigator I often used for background checks, among other things, and have him take a look. As for right now, I'd look at Taliyah Carter's social media sites. Maybe something there would give me a better idea of who I was dealing with.

That meant I had no time to deal with Hanna. She would just have to wait.

I ignored the implications that came with the sense of relief I felt at the thought.

Chapter 18

Hanna

I really didn't want to become one of those women who demanded their boyfriends call them every day or got upset when they weren't in constant contact. I'd never been like that.

But I couldn't deny that I was beyond normal frustration that I hadn't heard from Cross since I left his place Friday night. I thought he intended to call me Saturday late afternoon after the brunch, but when he hadn't, I assumed he just hadn't known when I'd be done. So I called him.

Twice.

I left two voicemails and received no responses. No texts. And not just on Saturday. I had no communication at all from him on Sunday either.

I refused to call him again. I wasn't going to be the woman who chased after the man. This was supposed to be an equal partnership. The two of us working together. Most people thought a Dom / Sub relationship was all about one person being in charge and bossing the other one around, but it was actually more of a balance than most other relationships. Ours always had been that way...but now, I felt like something was shifting between us.

Like I was the one reaching for him, wanting him more than he wanted me.

Not sexually, because he'd made it clear on Friday night that he was eager to indulge in as much of that part of our relationship as possible.

It was everything else that seemed to be falling apart.

Back when we first met, he'd made the distinction between lovers and sexual partners and had told me that I was the former. I'd never doubted it...until now. He'd said that what made the difference was the relationship beyond sex, and that had been true for us.

Except over the past couple weeks, things between us had been small talk and sex, nothing more. We seemed to be moving backwards, each day taking us further and further apart. The fact that he didn't want to talk to me this weekend only supported my fears.

I pushed myself back from my desk and stood. I leaned backward, wincing as my spine cracked and popped. For the past two hours, I'd been trying to concentrate on all of the notes I always made after an event, but I hadn't done much more than a few sentences. Every time I'd start to write, I'd find myself trailing off, staring at my screen, lost in some memory or another.

I wasn't sure which was worse, recalling the good times we'd had together, or remembering the fights. The worst, however, I knew without a doubt, was the current silence. The not knowing where we stood, what he was thinking or wanting.

And my pride wouldn't let me make the next move. I'd already done that. Twice. If he wanted to talk to me, he could call me back like he should have yesterday or the day before.

A not-so-small part of me thought I sounded petty

and immature, like I thought I was too good to try to make amends. I kept reminding myself that I hadn't done anything wrong, that Cross was the one who'd made everything weird, who was acting like a child.

I needed to get my mind off it, and work certainly wasn't cutting it. I walked around my desk and out into the lobby. Elora gave me a smile as I glanced in Juliette's office. No one was there, so I headed to the back. The chefs all had today off, so the only person back here was my sister.

"Taking inventory?" I asked as I walked toward her.

She nodded without turning toward me. "With everything that went crazy on Saturday, I didn't feel like doing it then. We didn't have anything on the schedule for today, so I figured it could wait until now."

Juliette trusted her employees, but we both knew that people sometimes forgot to write things down, or they used a little more of something than they thought. Which meant someone needed to do an inventory to count up everything on hand before our next event. Sometimes I did it, but sometimes she did. She said it relaxed her.

"How's it looking?" I asked.

"Pretty accurate," she said.

Not really a surprise. We were rarely off by too much.

I hadn't come back here to talk with her about the inventory though. Actually, I hadn't come back to talk to her about anything, really. She hadn't wanted to talk about Dalton or the baby even after the brunch was over, and I hadn't pushed. I didn't want her turning it on me and asking why I hadn't been with Cross.

I wasn't going to bring either subject up at the moment, so I simply went to stand by her side and watched her count. I had a feeling that she was feeling a lot of the same things I was. Confusion. Uncertainty. Neither of us had any idea of what our futures would hold, what decisions we were going to make about our current issues.

"I need an assistant," Juliette broke the silence. "You're doing great as the business manager, but right now, the two of us are picking up the slack that an assistant would usually deal with."

She didn't mention that, if she kept the baby, I'd need an assistant to help me keep things running while she was on maternity leave. I didn't say anything about it either.

"I put up some ads last week," she said. "And made a couple calls yesterday, so there are some people coming in to interview today and tomorrow. I sent you an email before I came in here."

"Why do you want me to do the interviews? It's for your assistant."

She glanced at me and raised an eyebrow.

Right. Stupid question.

Her last assistant had tried to kill her by cutting the brakes on one of the delivery vans, and when that failed, she'd arranged to have Juliette kidnapped. It made sense that my sister didn't trust her instincts when it came to that particular position.

"I'll take care of it."

She looked at me again. "You might want to go check that email."

I nodded and headed back toward my office. I was a little annoyed that she hadn't told me this last week, but there was no point in bringing it up now. Besides, neither one of us had been in the best frame of mind lately.

I'd taken half a dozen steps toward my office before I realized that Elora wasn't the only person in the lobby.

I was still staring when Tucker threw his arms

around me in a massive hug. For one strange moment, I was transported back in time.

"It will be all right, Hanna. You'll see."

Tucker pressed me even closer to his body, and I flushed. We'd had sex for the first time last night, and the feel of him made me remember every moment of it. I knew he hadn't been a virgin, but I'd been thankful for it when he'd taken my virginity without any of the awkward fumbling or pain I'd heard some of my classmates describe. I hadn't enjoyed it quite as much as I hoped I would, but I loved how close to him it made me feel.

And since he was heading off to Texas A&M while I was staying here in Ohio, I needed that reassurance. I'd started worrying about the long distance thing halfway through this year, and every time I heard someone talk about how high school sweethearts never stayed together, the sick feeling in my stomach had only gotten worse. I hadn't slept with him because I'd been worried that he'd find someone else to have sex with, and he hadn't pressured me to do it, but I would have been lying if I said the distance hadn't impacted my decision.

"You'll call me as soon as you get there?" I hated how weak my voice sounded.

He pulled back enough to look down at me. "I can't promise that. I don't know what time I'll get there, and then I have to get settled in my dorm."

"Text me at least then, so I know you got there safe."

He nodded. "I'll do that."

"Thank you."

He kissed my forehead. "Anything to make you happy."

I leaned into him, tightening my arms around his waist. We could do this. I knew we could. We could beat the odds. We'd see each other every break and over the summer. Get engaged probably Christmas of junior year, maybe just before senior year. Marriage shortly after graduation so that we could move to wherever the best job was. I was indifferent about staying in Zanesville, but Tucker was adamant. He wanted out.

Maybe that was what scared me so much. My older sister, Juliette, had wanted out of Ohio, and I hadn't seen her much since she'd gone to California. I didn't want that to happen to Tucker and me. I loved him.

I sucked in a breath and took a step back, freeing myself from his embrace as reality came crashing back in on me. I didn't love Tucker. Not anymore. I sometimes wondered if I really ever had.

"Hanna." Tucker beamed at me, completely oblivious to the shocked expression on Elora's face. "It's great to see you again. I'm sorry we didn't get to spend much time together when we saw each other over Thanksgiving."

"Um...uh..." Words seemed to have deserted me.

Elora came to my rescue. "Mr. Flannagan is here for his interview."

"Interview?" I looked at her, my brain trying to process the statement she'd just made.

"For the position of Juliette's assistant," she prompted.

I was going to kill my sister.

Why the *hell* had she thought it would be okay to bring in my ex-boyfriend to interview to be her assistant?

I was starting to suspect that her wanting me to take care of the interviews had less to do with my comfort level with her assistant, and more to do with the man standing in front of me.

"Didn't Juliette tell you I was coming in?" Tucker asked.

I forced a smile. "No, but that's all right." I gestured toward my office. "Right this way."

"I'm so glad she offered to let me apply for this job," he said as he followed me into my office. "I was worried I'd show up here in LA and not know anyone, not have a job..."

"Did you bring your resumé?" I half-expected him to give a typical Tucker response. Something like how he didn't need a resumé because he was so charming. Instead, he held out a piece of paper.

I sat down and took a few minutes to gather myself before reading the paper I held. It was odd, I thought, how thoughtless Tucker was all those years ago, and how much he'd changed...and how Cross had changed for the worse in just a few weeks. At least, when Tucker had acted like an ass, he'd been an eighteen-year-old frat boy, not a thirty-year-old wealthy CEO.

The interview went better than I'd expected, but I was still waiting in Juliette's office, annoyed, when she came in to get her things for lunch.

"What the hell, Juliette?"

She folded her arms and raised an eyebrow. "I didn't see any reason not to help him."

"The fact that he dumped me because he couldn't handle a long distance relationship wasn't good enough?"

"You said you were over it."

141

Shit. I had said that. And I was over it.

"Besides," Juliette continued with a smile. "I figured it might be a good idea for Cross to know that he better get his shit together because he's not the only fish in the sea."

I frowned. Well, damn. How was I supposed to be mad when she put it that way?

Chapter 19

Cross

I set down my phone and glared at it. I'd called Mars yesterday, and he'd agreed to look into Taliyah, but after checking in with him just now, he'd gotten nothing done. It'd taken almost all of my self-control not to snap at him when he'd reminded me that he had other clients he also had to answer to. Considering that my case wasn't exactly time sensitive, I couldn't be angry at him for not having results.

Or at least I shouldn't be.

I pinched the bridge of my nose and muttered a litany of curses under my breath. Part of me just wanted to call Taliyah and demand a DNA test, but I hadn't gotten to where I was by being impatient. I didn't rush into things. I thought things through. Planned. Weighed the pros and cons.

Was that, I wondered, the reason things with Hanna were so screwed up right now? Approaching her at the Breashears' event when I'd thought she was Juliette had been planned out. I'd considered all of the angles.

Well, all of them except for the one where I fell for the other sister.

No one could've planned for that.

Something about Hanna had made me abandon my usual caution so I could take care of her, so I could have her. If I'd been thinking with my head instead of other parts of my anatomy, I would've kept her at arm's length until I looked into her background, found out what type of person she was.

If I'd done that, however, I knew there was a good chance that I wouldn't have gotten involved with her at all. I would've thought she was too much of a risk. Too innocent. Too inexperienced. Nothing even close to what I was looking for.

I shook my head as a bitter laugh came out of me. That seemed to be my theme lately. Things I thought I wanted being turned completely on their head to become something I hadn't been looking for at all.

Hanna as a girlfriend.

Taliyah as a sister.

While I loved my parents, and I loved being the sole focus of their attention, after their deaths, I realized how much easier it would've been to have had someone else to go through it all with, to have someone who knew what I was going through. More importantly, if I had a sibling, I would still have a family.

Fate, it seemed, had a bit of a sharp sense of humor, giving me a sister in a way that made me see my parents in a new light, that made me question the life I'd experienced growing up.

More than anything, I wanted to talk to someone about this...no, that wasn't the truth. I didn't just want to talk to just anyone. I wanted to talk to Hanna. Wanted to confide in her, have her comfort me, give me advice. I wanted her to support me through this.

But I couldn't ask her to do that. Not when I'd balked at giving her that when I thought she was pregnant. I'd been there for her when we first met, but that was completely different. A situation I could control.

A situation that didn't really affect the direction I had planned for my life.

Those plans were starting to weigh on me now. I'd always assumed Hanna and I were on the same page, but I was starting to think that wasn't the case. I didn't want to talk about it yet though. I needed to get this thing with Taliyah settled first.

I hadn't been able to find out much about her on my own. She had social media sites but didn't include much personal information on them. At least not the kind I was looking for.

They confirmed that she was from Nashville, but I knew that was easily faked. People could put down whatever city of origin they wanted, and there was generally very little done to check it.

She had pictures of her and friends, but none of her mother. Not that a picture of her mother would prove anything. Liars came in all shapes and sizes. So did mistresses, one-night stands, and everything in-between. I wouldn't even be able to tell if she was my father's type. I knew from personal experience that a connection between two people had the power to override whatever someone may have thought of as their type.

My intercom buzzed.

"Mr. Phillips?"

"Yes?"

"You have a call on line two."

My heart lurched painfully as I immediately thought of Hanna. Had she decided to call me at work so I'd have to make an effort to ignore her? I wasn't really a believer in fate or destiny of any of that, but a part of me wondered if one of those were at work, forcing my hand with Hanna.

"Thank you. I'll take it from here." I took a moment to collect myself and then picked up the phone. "Hello?"

"Cross?"

A woman's voice, but not the one I wanted to hear.

"Taliyah."

"Hi." She sounded almost embarrassed. "Listen, I wanted to apologize for how everything went down on Friday. I came on really strong, and I had no right to do that. I don't want you to be angry with me for my mother having an affair with our father, so I never should've taken out on you how I felt about him."

I wasn't sure I liked her saying *our father*, like there was definitive proof that we shared a parent, but I had to admit that I appreciated her apology for the way she introduced herself. It made me think better of her and made me feel like I might be able to believe her.

"Thank you," I said. "You have to understand that this blind-sided me. I had absolutely no idea that you existed."

"I know," she said on a long sigh. "And I'm sure guys like you often have people claiming to be some long-lost relative."

A little of the weight lifted from my shoulders. She understood why I was hesitating. "All the time," I said. "Which is why we can never be too careful."

"It's half past eleven," she said, "and I'm shopping not too far from you. Would you like to have lunch?"

I didn't even have to think about it. "That sounds good." Maybe a bit more time with her in a more relaxed, informal setting would get me some of the answers I was looking for. "Want to meet me at Ammo on North Highland in twenty?"

"That sounds perfect." Relief was evident in each

word. "I'll see you there."

As the call ended, I buzzed Abraham. "Call Ammo and get me one of their private booths. There'll be two of us for lunch today."

"Yes, sir."

I turned my attention back to my computer, thinking I'd be able to concentrate now that I had a plan set to talk with Taliyah. Before I'd gotten more than a couple sentences into the paragraph I was reading. However, my cell phone vibrated, letting me know I had a text message.

Want to meet for lunch today?

Hanna.

It was abrupt, without any endearments, which alone was enough to tell me that she was upset and that she most likely wanted this lunch so we could talk. Even if I hadn't already made plans with Taliyah, I wouldn't have been ready to talk to her. I wasn't sure when that would be.

I can't. Working through today. Maybe tomorrow.

A few seconds later, her reply came back.

Busy tomorrow. Let me know when you're free.

I winced at how abrupt it sounded but knew that the only way to fix the mess between us was to get things straightened out with Taliyah, so I could focus on Hanna. And the next step to that was lunch.

"Thank you for agreeing to meet with me again," Taliyah said as she slid into the seat across from me.

She looked different than she had before. Not that she'd changed her hair or anything. It was more in the way she carried herself. The arrogance she'd had when she'd come into my office was still there, but it was...dimmed. I didn't know if she was purposefully turning it down, or if she'd genuinely had some sort of epiphany, but it didn't really matter.

"We got off on the wrong foot," she continued.

I gave a shrug. "It's not like there's a handbook on how to do this."

"Maybe we should write one," she joked. Her eyes danced with amusement. *"101 Ways to Tell Someone You're Their Sister."*

I couldn't help but laugh. "Quite the niche market."

"And there'd always be the possibility of sequels," she continued. "It could be a whole series. Brother, father, mother, daughter, son."

"I can see the marketing now. 'Do you need to tell someone that the two of you are related, but don't know how?'"

"They could be marketed to some of those talk shows that are always playing the whole 'whose your daddy' game," she suggested.

If my parents were still alive, we most likely wouldn't have been joking like this, but at the moment, it seemed like the best way to diffuse the tension. And it worked. I felt more relaxed at the moment than I had in a while.

"Can I ask you a question?" I figured I might as well give it a shot. Her answer might not be the truth, but I could use it to measure against whatever Mars found to gauge how honest she was being with me.

"Sure." She took a drink of whatever fruity concoction she'd ordered.

148

On my way here, I considered what I'd ask her if I got the chance, which question would be the most important, the one I absolutely had to make sure I asked her in case she got angry at me for asking it. In the end, there was one that I felt like I had to know.

"Why now?" I asked. "It seems like you knew who our father was from a young age. I could see waiting until you were eighteen, or after college, or even right after he died. But why'd you come to me now?"

She considered the question. I wasn't sure if that was a good thing or a bad one. She could be thinking about what lie to tell, or she could be actually thinking about how best to answer the question. Sometimes motives weren't so cut and dry as people wanted to believe.

"I thought about it all the time when I was younger," she said slowly. "Just showing up on his doorstep and announcing who I was. I knew you existed, and for a long time, I even hated you for getting to live the perfect, privileged life."

I didn't interrupt to argue with her. She was telling me what I wanted to know, not what I wanted to hear. I couldn't be upset if they weren't the same thing.

"By the time I was in college, I'd come to peace with it," she continued, a wry smile on her face. "Or at least I thought I had. I didn't think anything of it until I saw the article in the paper that he'd died."

I felt a faint stab of grief, but my sorrow over the death of my parents was no longer as sharp as it once had been. I missed them, but it wasn't the same.

"I thought about coming to see you then, telling you who I was." She locked her eyes with mine. "But I couldn't do that to you. As an adult, I understood that it wasn't your fault, none of it. And even though we'd both lost our father, you'd lost a person you had a relationship with. I'd only lost the idea of a father. A concept."

The negative emotions I'd felt toward Taliyah started to soften. Everything that she was saying made sense.

"I tried to forget about it again," she went on. "I told myself that it didn't matter because I'd never have a chance to meet him now, but I couldn't stop thinking about you."

"It's been eight years since he passed," I said. I didn't make it a question, but I knew she understood what I was asking.

She swallowed hard. "Eighteen months ago, my mother was diagnosed with cancer."

My stomach sank. I was pretty sure I knew what was coming next, and it would explain everything, including the way she'd come across the first time we met.

"She never married," Taliyah said. "Never had any other kids. So it was just me and her through all of it. My grandparents both died when I was still a kid, so when Mom passed a couple months ago..." She let her voice trail off, but I didn't need her to finish the sentence. I knew how it ended.

Alone.

Like I was.

Maybe she wasn't so different from me after all.

Chapter 20

Hanna

A full week, and the extent of the conversation between Cross and myself had been a series of back and forth texts about how neither of us had the time to meet for lunch or dinner. We were falling apart, and I didn't know how to stop it. Hell, I didn't even know if Cross wanted to stop it.

I supposed I'd find out tonight. We finally agreed to meet for dinner, which I hoped meant that we were finally going to discuss what was going on between us. I couldn't keep doing this indefinitely. Juliette would be making a lot of important decisions in the near future, and I couldn't let myself be distracted by whatever personal shit was going on in my life.

Juliette was more important than anything else. Her and that baby. Cross hadn't promised a future where he was more to me than what he was now. And while I loved him, he wasn't family. His words and actions were making that abundantly clear.

I didn't go straight from work. In fact, I took off an hour early after handing over the five most promising resumés to Juliette. I didn't want to see a smug smile when she saw that Tucker was one of them.

He really was one of the most qualified applicants I'd met with all week.

I told Juliette that I wanted some extra time to get ready for my date. She knew things were rocky with us, so she told me to go. Now I was standing in front of the full length mirror in my bedroom and double-checking the outfit I'd finally chosen for tonight.

I'd bought the dress before we'd gone to Ohio, but hadn't had the opportunity to wear it. Tonight seemed like the perfect night.

It was velvet, a deep, rich purple that made my eyes look darker, my skin more translucent. It had three-quarters sleeves, but was off the shoulder and exposed the tops of my breasts. The hem was mid-thigh, modest enough for me to wear a thong without worrying about how much flesh I might flash.

My gaze fell on the box on my dresser. Cross hadn't asked me to wear my collar, but I reached for the box anyway. If tonight was about deciding where we were going in our relationship, then he needed a reminder of exactly what he'd promised me, of what we'd promised each other. If we were going to end this tonight, we would do it with our eyes open.

I squared my shoulders, shook out my curls, and then headed out the door. Cross often insisted that he provide me with a car when we were meeting places, but not today. I took a cab to our favorite restaurant and was shown to our usual quiet back booth. Cross was already there, completely absorbed in something on his phone. He didn't even look up until the hostess cleared her throat.

I wasn't a suspicious person by nature, not really, but alarm bells were going off as his head jerked up and he quickly shoved his phone into his pocket. Something that looked an awful lot like guilt flashed across his face, and then it was gone, smothered by appreciation and desire as he looked at me.

I slid into the booth and waited for him to meet me half-way. When he did, he leaned down to kiss my cheek. I told myself it was because he didn't want to risk smudging my lipstick, or wearing it, but I didn't think it boded well for the rest of the evening.

"You look lovely," he said. "Is that a new dress?"

"It is," I answered.

He reached over and ran his finger over my collar, and I shivered. It was an innocuous touch, nothing anyone would really think anything of, but I felt it go straight through me. He leaned closer so that his lips were pressed against my ear.

"You're wearing your collar."

"Yes, Sir." I kept my voice low.

Before he could say anything else, our wine arrived, and he was distracted by offering his approval. When he turned back to me, the moment had faded. I knew it was still there since his eyes would occasionally flick up to the collar, but he didn't mention it again. Instead, he turned the conversation to mundane things.

"You've been pretty busy at work this week," he said. "What does Juliette have you working on so hard."

"Finding an assistant," I answered honestly. "I narrowed down the pool of candidates by doing interviews all week."

I didn't tell him that one of the finalists was my ex. No need to bring any of that up when things were already tense between us.

"Has she made any decisions about the pregnancy?" he asked without looking at me.

"Not yet. She did tell the father, and she wants him to

be part of the decision making."

Cross was quiet for a moment, and I wondered if he was thinking about his own reaction when he thought he was on that end of things. I knew we needed to talk about our problems, but I didn't want to bring that whole fiasco up right now.

The silence stretched between us, so I filled it with the first thing that came to mind. "Juliette wants us to go out with her and Dalton tomorrow night."

"Dalton?"

With that one word, I realized just how long it'd been since we'd really talked. I hadn't told him about Dalton. "He's the father."

"Oh."

More uncomfortable silence.

"What about you?" I asked, following his conversational lead. "A whole week of working through lunches. Must be important."

I was pleased that none of my negative emotions bled through. I wanted to know what was going on, but I didn't want him on the defensive.

"Nothing interesting," he said. "Just a lot of tedious stuff that needed to get done."

Another long break of silence. This wasn't going the way I'd hoped, and the rest of the dinner pretty much went the same way.

It wasn't until we were walking away from the table that he put his hand on the small of my back and leaned in close. "Come back to my place." His fingers flexed. "I've missed you."

My body tightened. I'd missed him too.

154

The collar Cross had made for me had unique twists that allowed for clips to be fastened to it for various forms of bondage. At the moment, I had two chains connecting my collar to the sides of the padded bench I was currently bent over.

As soon as we'd gotten into the house, Cross had ordered me to strip to nothing but my strapless bra and the matching lavender thong. And my collar, of course. Then he'd kissed me the entire way to the playroom so that we were both breathless by the time we closed the door.

He'd taken off my bra then, licking and sucking on my nipples until they were hard and throbbing. Now, they were aching even more because he'd fastened his favorite pair of nipple clamps on them before binding me to the bench.

He ran his hand over my ass before bringing it down on my cheek hard enough to make me gasp. The movement of my ribs made the clamps on my nipples sway, sending new jolts of pain through my breasts. I closed my eyes, letting myself slip into that place where subs often went during a scene, where they gave themselves over with complete abandon. When the next few strikes landed on my ass, I absorbed the sting, the heat, drew it into myself, added it to the pain and pleasure.

I felt him draw aside my thong and trace along my slit. When he parted my folds and caressed the tip of my clit, I moaned. It was a brief touch, and then he was pushing two fingers inside me. Before I could adjust, his free hand was back on my ass, spanking me even as he twisted his fingers. Short, brutal thrusts matched in time with enough blows to make my skin tingle and burn.

At least I wouldn't have to worry about being embarrassed tomorrow night when it was difficult to sit. Juliette and Dalton would completely get it.

Cross's fingers pressed hard against my g-spot, and I saw stars. As he rubbed it, amping up the pressure building inside me, he reached beneath me and tugged on one of my nipple clamps.

I wailed as I came, long past any self-consciousness when it came to responding to him. Unless I'd been given specific instructions not to make a sound, I didn't hold back.

I whimpered as he pulled his fingers out, shudders still rolling through my body. I expected to feel his cock next, but I didn't. Instead, he disappeared for a moment, and when he returned, he ran the soft leather strips from his favorite flogger across my back. He didn't use it often, and even more rarely, after he'd spanked me. He flicked it against my back, moving across my shoulders and down my spine, no blow hard enough to hurt.

Then he moved to the side and brought the flogger up against my breasts. My entire body jerked, the chains holding me down tightened at my response. It hadn't been a cruel blow, but it'd jostled the clamps, and that had hurt. He did it two more times, and I flinched at each one.

"Let's get those off you," he said quietly as he reached down and removed one clamp, then the other.

I shivered at the pins and needles moving through my sensitive flesh as blood flow returned. The shivers became cries as Cross resumed the use of his flogger on my breasts.

"Please, Cross," I begged. A harder strike made me remember what I was supposed to call him. "Please, Sir."

"Please what?"

"Please, fuck me, Sir."

156

"Do your tits hurt, baby?" He reached down to squeeze one.

I strangled back a cry and managed. "Yes."

"Is that why you want me to stop?"

"No." I shook my head as much as I could with the collar locked in place. "I need you to fuck me."

When he moved behind me, I breathed a sigh of relief. Everything he'd been doing had me dancing the razor's edge of arousal, that nearly painful point that he loved to draw out as long as possible.

The sensation of something hard and unyielding pressing against my entrance snapped my thoughts back into place. I gasped, tensed, then relaxed as Cross put his hand on my lower back.

"Relax, baby. The handle isn't much bigger than I am. I know you can take it."

Handle? My eyes flew open as I realized what Cross was working deeper into me. The hard leather handle of his flogger. We'd used plugs and dildos in the past, but never this. It felt different, not necessarily bad, but as he said, it was bigger than him, and that was saying a lot.

I closed my eyes again and focused on the myriad feelings rippling out from where my pussy clung to leather. He made a few strokes with it, letting me adjust to the girth and length, then pushed it all the way inside. He left it there as he came around to stand in front of me.

He'd taken off his clothes at some point, so his thick erection was right in front of my mouth. He didn't even have to give the command, and I was parting my lips. The head slid across my tongue, leaving the salty taste of his precum in its wake. He fisted his hands in my hair, letting me know that he wanted to do the work. If I needed to use my safe word while my mouth was full, I'd have to resort to the other signal we'd set up: me snapping my fingers.

157

I wasn't really thinking about any of that though. My mind was consumed with the way my pussy was pulsing around the handle in it, with the taste and weight of him as he fucked my mouth. He didn't push too far or try to force me to take him deeper than I usually did. I kept up the suction as best I could and tried to keep from wiggling around to see if I could get the friction I needed to go over the edge.

"Swallow it all," he said, his voice rough. "And I'll let you come again."

I glanced up at him to let him know I understood, and then he was coming. His hips jerked against my face, hands tightening painfully in my hair even as he pulsed and twitched in my mouth. I swallowed even as I used my tongue and lips to draw out every last drop, working over the sensitive flesh until he pulled away.

I drew in a harsh gasp of air and watched him disappear from sight. A moment later, the handle inside me twisted as it withdrew. I moaned as he repeated the action over and over until I was finally there, crying out his name and coming hard enough for things to go gray.

When I came to, I was on the bed in the playroom. I'd been cleaned up and tucked in, but Cross wasn't there. I heard the shower from the connecting bathroom and sat up, wincing as the fabric rubbed against my skin. Yeah, dinner tomorrow was going to be fun.

Now came the big decision. Did I stay the night, spend tomorrow with Cross before the double-date with Juliette and Dalton, or did I leave him a note and go home? We hadn't talked yet, but I wasn't sure I wanted to do that right after sex, or tomorrow right before the date. Neither one seemed like good options.

I was still debating what to do when I heard a phone buzz. I automatically reached for it, not realizing that I'd grabbed Cross's instead of mine until I saw an unfamiliar name on the screen.

Taliyah.

I've really enjoyed getting to know you over lunch this past week. Maybe we can do dinner sometime. I really hope that this relationship can move forward into something great.

What the fuck?

Chapter 21

Cross

I was surprised when I came out of the shower and found the playroom empty, but I assumed she'd just decided to use one of the other showers instead of waiting for me to finish. Except she wasn't in any of them. Next, I tried the kitchen to see if she might have gotten hungry for some sort of dessert or needed something to drink. But she wasn't there either.

I went back upstairs and grabbed my phone. She answered on the second ring.

"Yes?"

Her voice was so cold that it caught me off guard. The questions I'd intended to ask, about where she was and why she'd left, died in my mouth.

"What time do you want me to pick you up tomorrow?"

There was a moment of silence before she answered, "Five-thirty. We're meeting Juliette and Dalton at six."

And that was the end of the conversation. My sexual appetite was sated for the moment, but I was still restless. I'd gotten used to having Hanna with me most nights, and always over the weekend. Whether we were having plain, vanilla sex, or indulging in something a bit more kinky, we were together. Before I met her, I'd never spent more than a couple nights with the same woman. I hadn't seen the appeal. Now, I did, and it seemed like, unless something changed, I'd be heading back to my old habits soon.

It was that thought that kept me up all night, that kept my stomach in knots all day. I wanted to call her, ask her why she'd left so abruptly, but I couldn't deny that my pride was hurt. She clearly had something going on that she didn't want to talk to me about, something that she either felt she couldn't trust me with or that she was too angry to speak about. And in a relationship that was supposed to be based on trust, her lack of it in me hurt.

It was almost lunch when I remembered that Taliyah had texted me yesterday, and I hadn't responded. Talking to her was as good a way as any to distract myself. It'd worked before.

So for the next few hours, I found a game on television and texted my sister. Or, my half-sister. If she was telling the truth. When I first met her, I wasn't sure if I'd wanted her to be lying or not. Now, I was leaning toward wanting it to be the truth. No matter if Taliyah was related to me or not, I knew that my father had cheated on my mother. I might as well get some family out of the deal.

I was so caught up in my conversation that I didn't notice the time until my calendar notification went off, reminding me that I had a date to get ready for. I told Taliyah that I had to go, turned off the game I'd only half been paying attention to, and headed to my bedroom to get dressed.

I went with a fitted shirt and nice pair of pants, ran a

hand through my hair, and then headed down to decide which car to take. I was in the mood to drive tonight. And a bit recklessly, I realized as I started toward Vine Street.

Hanna looked as lovely as ever as she answered her door. She was wearing another new dress, this one dark blue. It clung to her breasts and hips. I leaned down and kissed her cheek even though every bone in my body wanted a different sort of kiss. Something deep and passionate, the sort of kiss that would take us to the bedroom and keep us there all night.

But this wasn't the time or place for it.

"Ready?" I asked.

She nodded but didn't look at me as she stepped past. Whatever I thought I felt from her last night wasn't in my head. She was pissed about something. I just couldn't figure out for the life of me what it was.

I followed her, got ahead to open the car door. Our drive to the restaurant was quiet, the tension between us thick, and it didn't ease when we arrived at our destination. Fortunately, Juliette was already there, sitting next to a man who looked about my age, and both looking as uncomfortable as I felt.

This was going to be a pleasant dinner.

As we sat down, Juliette introduced the man to me, and we ordered our drinks. The small talk was nearly painful, but we all kept it up. Juliette and I had become friends over the past few months, though judging by the way she looked at me, that friendship wouldn't last long if I didn't fix things with Hanna.

"How long have the two of you been together?" Dalton asked as we waited for our appetizers.

"Almost six months," Hanna answered. Her voice was easy enough, but she didn't look at me. "I'm surprised the two of you haven't met. What with everyone traveling in the same circles."

Dalton glanced at me, and I watched as he placed my name. It wasn't a surprise that I'd never met him before. He was a straight, male Sub, and I was a straight, male Dom. We didn't exactly partner up with the same people, and when we went to a club looking for someone to spend time with, neither one of us would've been looking for the other.

"I've heard of you," he said finally. "You have quite the reputation."

I wasn't sure if that was a good thing or a bad thing.

"Yes, he does," Hanna muttered.

That definitely sounded like a bad thing.

Before I could ask about it though, our party of four suddenly became a party of five when an unfortunately familiar person approached.

Tucker.

I ground my teeth together and resisted the urge to punch him on principle alone.

"Hanna, Juliette, it's great to see you both again."

"Tucker." Juliette's smile was warm. "This is Dalton and Cross." She gestured toward me.

"Nice to meet you." Dalton reached across the table to extend a hand.

I held out my own but didn't bother with a greeting.

"I'm not checking up on my interview," Tucker said with a grin. "I promise. Just wanted to come over and say hi to the few friendly faces I know in the city."

Interview. He was one of the people Hanna had interviewed for the position of Juliette's assistant.

And she hadn't told me a thing about it.

My temper started to bubble up.

"You look great, Hanna."

I clenched my hands into fists as he leaned closer to

her. If we were at the club, no one would've dared to approach her while she was with me. Actually, I didn't know many men with balls big enough to come near her when she was with me in any setting.

Except she hadn't said who I was to her.

And she wasn't pushing him away, wasn't making a point of letting him know that she was off-limits.

"Excuse me," I muttered as I stood. I needed to leave, or I would do or say something I'd regret.

I walked toward the back without looking at anyone, but I felt her behind me. Hanna was following, but I didn't stop until we were in the small alcove near the restrooms. Only then did I turn and face her.

"Is there something you'd like to say?" I snapped.

"There are quite a few things I'd like to say," she retorted, putting her hands on her hips. "But at the moment, I'd just like to know if you're going to spend the rest of the evening with a stick up your ass."

I scowled down at her. "Maybe Tucker's more pleasant company."

"Tucker?" Her eyes narrowed. "You're really going to play that card? Seriously?"

"He's your ex-boyfriend, and I didn't hear you telling him that you were seeing someone."

"Did you tell Taliyah?"

I blinked in surprise. "What?" I hadn't expected that.

"Taliyah. Last night, I picked up your phone by mistake, and I saw a text from the woman you've been spending your lunches with. Lunches you told me you couldn't have with me because you were working through them. But you were actually with some other woman–"

My temper snapped. "She's my *sister*, Hanna."

165

Chapter 22

Hanna

Of all the possible responses I'd imagined Cross giving when I finally confronted him about Taliyah, this was definitely not one of them. He had no family, and certainly not a sister. He told me that himself not long after we met.

"Say that again?" I had an idea that I sounded like an idiot, but I needed to hear him say the words one more time so I could make sure I heard him correctly. Then I needed to know what the hell was going on here.

"Taliyah is my sister," he said it slower this time. "Half-sister, actually."

A thousand thoughts swirled through my head, but the one I knew I had to get out first was an apology. "I'm sorry. I didn't know. I should've given you the benefit of the doubt."

He nodded, then reached for my hand. He pulled me to him, raising my hand to his face so he could kiss my palm. "And I'm sorry for snapping about Tucker. I was jealous."

I let him wrap his arms around me, and as I pressed my face against his chest, I allowed myself to relax, to feel the same sense of safety I felt when I first met him.

He'd taken care of me then, protected me. I'd known that nothing could touch me as long as he was there.

I wanted that back. I wanted to make this work.

"We should probably head back before Dalton thinks we don't like him." Cross's voice held a teasing note that I hadn't heard in a while. I'd missed it.

"And your sister?" I didn't want him to think that I'd forgotten or that I didn't care. I wanted to know what was going on with him. And why he hadn't come to me about her in the first place.

"Later," he said. "I promise. Right now, I'd like to make sure Tucker knows that you're taken."

He kept his arm around my waist as we walked back to the table, and I felt some of my anxiety ebb. It wasn't completely gone, and I knew it wouldn't be until Cross and I had a much longer discussion about our recent string of miscommunications, but I at least felt like we could proceed with dinner in a much more comfortable fashion.

Which I was sure we would...once Tucker left. He'd definitely noticed the possessive grip Cross had on me. He'd smiled at us, but I still knew him well enough to see that it hadn't reach his eyes.

"Are you here with someone, Tucker?" Cross asked as he pulled out my chair for me. "Because if the two of you would like to join us, I'm sure I could get us a bigger table."

Something dark flashed across Tucker's face, and then it was gone, quick enough that I almost thought I imagined it.

"That's okay," he said with a tight smile. "I just wanted to come over and say hi." He looked at Juliette and then at me. "I'll see you around."

As Tucker left, Dalton spoke up, "I feel like I came

in in the middle of something."

I glanced at Juliette, and she shrugged. Apparently, it was up to me to decide how much Dalton knew. "Tucker's my ex-boyfriend from back in Ohio. He just moved out here."

Dalton's dark blue-gray eyes slid from me to Cross and back again. Then he changed the subject. "So, did you always want to go into business on your own?"

And with that, the conversation moved to easier topics. We discussed our childhood, the differences between Hollywood and Zanesville – of which there were many – and other various things that helped us get to know each other without venturing into anything particularly painful.

It didn't take me long to see what Juliette had seen in Dalton. I knew my sister well enough to know that it wasn't Dalton's pretty face that had attracted her to him. He was sweet and funny, with a confidence that some may have found off-putting in a Sub, but that I knew Juliette liked. In some ways, he even reminded me of myself, able to care for himself, but with a desire to be able to hand all of that control over to someone else.

I told Juliette that I'd support whatever decision she made, and I intended to stick to that, but I couldn't help hoping that she and Dalton would try to make a go of it. She might not think about settling down, but I could see how good he could be for her. And the more I listened to him talk, the more I knew our parents would be thrilled to have him dating Juliette.

As long as they never found out exactly how they met.

"So if you were raised in Northern California and went to Vanderbilt, how'd you end up in LA?" Cross asked. "You don't want to be an actor or anything like that?"

Dalton shook his head as he swallowed the bite of cod he'd just taken. "I've always wanted to be a teacher, and while I was finishing up my Masters, one of my professors mentioned that his alma mater was in need of elementary level teachers. It sounded exactly like what I'd been looking for, so I asked him to make a call."

"What about your family?" I asked. "Didn't they want you to move closer to home?"

He gave me an easy smile. "LA's closer to home than Nashville was."

"Good point." I chuckled. "I hadn't thought about it that way."

"Besides," he continued. "They understood why I was doing what I was doing, and they supported me."

I glanced at Juliette and saw my own feelings mirrored in her eyes. It would have been nice to have family who was that understanding.

"I know you work with Juliette," Dalton directed his question to me. "Was that always the plan?"

It wasn't until he asked the question that I realized I didn't truly have an answer. I'd gotten my MBA but hadn't really known what I wanted to do with it. I supposed a part of me always assumed I'd end up in the auto shop, no matter what protests I made, and I figured that a degree would at least give me some leverage over how things were run. Then I'd gotten the offer to help Juliette, and some time away had seemed like a good idea, a way to put my degree to practical use. Again, so I'd have something to reference back in Ohio if anyone tried to pull the inexperience card. I'd never considered what I actually wanted to do.

And, not surprisingly, Dalton was the first person who'd ever asked me. Juliette had left before I'd decided anything about college, and Cross had met me after I'd already been working for Juliette. Them not asking me anything made sense, I supposed, but my parents hadn't bothered to talk to me about it either. Even my guidance counselor in high school had assumed I was going into the family business.

I shrugged. "Actually, I didn't really have a plan beyond coming out here, but I think Juliette and I are working well together."

"We are," she agreed.

The glance Juliette threw me said we were thinking the same thing. That it was a good thing I was here since she would most likely be needing all the extra support she could get over the next few months.

Dalton looked between Juliette and myself. "Okay, I'm probably going to get slapped for this, but I have to ask, what's the age difference here?"

Juliette laughed. "Depends on how old you think we are."

"Five years," I answered. "And we'll all just assume that you thought Juliette was younger."

Another laugh went around the table, and I felt a flash of hope. This could work. Dalton and Juliette together with their baby. Me working with her. Cross and I together. This could be our future.

"She found me the Monday after Thanksgiving." Cross broke the silence that had been between us ever

171

since we'd left the restaurant.

I didn't have to ask him who he was talking about. I just felt relief that he was telling me like he'd said he would, and without me having to prompt him.

"My dad had an affair with her mom," he continued.

I didn't interrupt as he told me the whole story, including his meeting with her during the lunches he said he was working. I was still a little pissed that he hadn't told me about her before, and that he'd lied to me about why he couldn't meet me for lunch, but I knew that wasn't what was important right now. We'd deal with my issues later. Right now, he needed me to support him.

"And we talked most of the day today," he said. "Mars is still looking into things, but I think I believe her."

I wanted to ask if she'd asked him for anything yet, but I knew he wouldn't take it well. He considered himself a good judge of character, and I knew that most of the time, that was accurate, but I didn't think that ability translated quite as well when it came to family. I knew how much he missed his parents, and Taliyah was a connection to them, a piece of family that he never thought he'd have.

"I'd be interested in meeting her."

It seemed like the safest thing to say at the moment. Besides, if I supported him, and was polite to her, anything I questioned once I got the measure of her myself would have more weight. Or at least I hoped it would. I didn't want to see him get hurt.

At that thought, a flash of anger went through me, hotter and brighter than anything I'd felt since Juliette had been taken. I didn't care who Taliyah was, I promised myself, if she hurt Cross, I'd make sure she suffered.

He took my hand as we walked into the house, lacing

our fingers together. I took comfort in the gesture, let it give me strength for what I knew was coming. I couldn't put it off any longer. I didn't want to. If there was any chance at all for us to have a future together, we needed to talk about the things that were still between us.

"Would you like some wine?" Cross asked as I closed the door behind us.

Alcohol sounded like a good way to start things off. We hadn't ordered any at dinner since Juliette couldn't drink, and I hadn't minded, but a bit of something to take the edge off at the moment would be nice.

"Yes, please." I kicked off my shoes and followed him into the kitchen, watching as he poured us both glasses of something that I was sure was quite expensive.

He handed me a glass and then leaned down to kiss me. I let myself enjoy the connection for a moment, but before it could become anything more, I took a step back. Cross frowned, and I took a sip of wine to steady my nerves.

"We need to talk," I said quietly. "We keep falling into bed together but never address any of the issues that have been building between us. We can't keep on going this way."

For a moment, I was afraid that he might refuse, that he'd tell me to leave. But he gave a curt nod, and I knew that it was time to lay all our cards on the table.

Chapter 23

Hanna

He really didn't want to talk. There was no doubt in my mind about that.

"What's wrong with the way things were going?" he asked as he leaned back against the counter. "We were comfortable together, weren't we?"

I nodded. "We were, but it could never last that way."

"Why not?" He at least sounded like he was asking an honest question rather than like a petulant child complaining. "Why can't we just go back to the way things used to be?"

"Because that's not what I want from our relationship," I answered honestly. "And I think that's what we need to talk about."

He sighed. "I think we should top off our glasses and have a seat in the living room."

He was right. I doubted this would be a pleasant conversation.

Less than five minutes later, we were settled on opposite ends of the couch, turned toward each other, wine glasses in hand.

He raised his toward me. "You wanted us to talk.

Let's get to it."

I took another drink, then went back to the matter at hand. "When I asked you to go to Ohio with me for Thanksgiving, I thought we were on the same page. You meeting my family, spending a holiday with us. If you hadn't wanted to, if you hadn't felt like you were ready for that, you could've just told me."

Cross's expression hardened. "I wanted to go with you. How could you think otherwise?"

"How?" I struggled to keep my voice even. "The fact that you completely freaked out when you thought I was pregnant seems to be a pretty good reason."

"There's a big difference between meeting your parents and thinking you're pregnant," he countered. "You can't blame me for being upset."

"That wasn't just upset." I wouldn't let him downplay it again. "You admitted that the things you said were awful, but you never talked about why you said them."

"I was upset."

I shook my head. "Not good enough. Those were nasty accusations." I swallowed hard, trying to push back the hurt so that I could think clearly. "They didn't sound like the man I thought I knew."

"You do know me." He started to reach toward me but then dropped his hand. "People say all kinds of things when they're upset."

"I didn't think you were that kind of man."

He frowned. "Is that what this is really about? I don't live up to some perfected ideal that you have, and suddenly everything we've been to each other doesn't mean shit?"

I leaned forward. "We're not talking about me finding out that you leave the toilet seat up or throw your wet towels on the floor. You were...mean, Cross." I

176

blinked back the tears that wanted to form.

He moved so that he was kneeling in front of me. "I'm so sorry for that. Really, I am."

"Then talk to me," I said. "Tell me why."

He took my hands as he moved up to the couch. "People like me, who have money and power, can be a target for manipulative people."

Taliyah's name flashed across my mind, but I didn't say it. If I brought up my suspicions about her, it'd shift the conversation, and right now, this was more important.

"I never should've put that on you," he continued. "It was unfair, and, yes, mean. There was absolutely no excuse for it."

"Thank you." We were getting somewhere, but I knew I still hadn't gotten quite to the bottom of things. There had to be more to it than just that. "Why did the pregnancy test set you off? Why that and not something else?"

He released my hands and moved away from me. "Just let it go, Hanna. Let's go back to the way things were before all of that happened. I'll never treat you like that again."

Part of me wanted to give in, to take him at his word, but I knew that, eventually, things would come to a head again. Better now than later.

"You said you didn't want anything to do with a family." I watched his expression carefully. "Isn't that really what triggered it? Thinking that you would have to face what you wanted from the future."

His eyes cut down, and I knew I'd gotten it right.

I pressed harder, needing to know how deep it went. If it was even worth trying to mend things. "Was it the thought of how things would have to change between us?" I forced myself to voice the newest fear. "That you

177

wouldn't...want me when I started to put on weight. After I had a baby."

His head jerked up, and he looked both startled and offended at the comments. "How could you think that?"

I raised an eyebrow. "Don't you remember what you said about Juliette? About how no one would want a pregnant dominatrix?" My voice cracked, and I flushed.

"No, no, baby, that's not it." He put his hand on my knee. "I didn't mean it like that. I wasn't talking about people in a relationship. I was talking about her clients. It's a totally different thing."

I felt a little better but still needed more reassurance. "So you weren't worried that you'd find me...unattractive if I were pregnant?"

He shook his head but took his hand off my knee. He was telling the truth, but I knew there was something he wasn't saying. Something I had to force myself to say.

"You just didn't like the idea of me being pregnant at all." My voice was soft. "That's it, isn't it? The thought of having kids, having a family..."

I looked at him, but he wouldn't look at me. All of my fears came flooding forward as I forced myself to admit that I was probably right.

"Have you thought about what you want from the future?" I asked. "Not only with us but in anything? Or has it always been about maintaining the status quo?"

His silence spoke volumes. Excruciating, heart-wrenching volumes.

"I'm not asking for anything specific," I continued even as my insides twisted and churned. "It's not that I think there's a place we're supposed to be at right now, or that I expect something to happen overnight, but...I need to know that we're going somewhere. That there will be more to this relationship than me keeping a few things here and staying over a couple nights a week."

This time, I didn't try to fill the quiet. I waited. We'd had too many assumptions between us, too many misunderstandings. Whatever happened now, I was determined that it would be done with both of us clearly understanding what was happening and why. I wouldn't let my fear of losing him keep me in a relationship that was going nowhere.

After a minute or two, he stood with a weary sigh. He walked over to the window without looking at me. "What do you want from me, Hanna?"

My knuckles turned white as I gripped my hands together. "I'm not putting anything on a timetable, but I want a family, Cross. I want marriage and kids someday."

"I thought you left Ohio to get away from those expectations."

I closed my eyes and let out a shaky breath. Everything was falling apart, and I knew there was nothing I could do to put it back together, but I had to be honest with him. We both deserved that. "I left so that I could be my own person, so I could decide for myself what I wanted."

"And a family is what you want." He didn't make it a question.

"Yes." I stood, unable to take sitting any longer. If things were ending, I'd face them on my feet. "And I'm sorry."

He glanced back at me. "For what?"

"For assuming that's what you wanted." I swallowed hard. "I should have let you know from moment one what I wanted and asked if we were on the same page. None of this would've happened if I'd just been upfront."

"What if I would've said that I didn't know what I wanted?" He turned around, his face pale and drawn.

179

"What if I wanted to see how things went before I decided what I wanted from the future?"

I wanted to tell him that it was okay, that I would wait with him to see where things went.

But I couldn't do it.

"I'd ask you if it was marriage and family that you wanted, or if it was just me."

He took a step toward me. "Isn't wanting you enough?"

Tears pricked my eyes, and I forced them back. "Not enough to have a family. You'd end up resenting me, resenting our family, and I can't do that. I couldn't bear to think that I'd trapped you in a life you didn't want, that you'd hate me, leave me with a family you never wanted."

"But I might want those things," he said, his eyes boring into mine. "I need time to think about it."

I wanted to believe him, wanted to believe that in a couple hours, he'd tell me that he wanted the same things, that he wanted us to move forward. I was honest when I said that I wasn't on a schedule. I didn't care if we didn't start talking marriage seriously for another couple years, but I had to know that it was on the table. I had to know that he wouldn't freak out if I talked about it like it was a relatively certain thing. I wasn't foolish enough to think that nothing would ever come between us, but I couldn't stay in a perpetual state of limbo, waiting for him to decide whether or not he wanted a family.

I loved him. There was no doubt in my mind about that. But I would end up hating him if I stayed with him and lost the family I wanted to have one day.

"Take all the time you need," I said quietly. "I want you to be happy, Cross, and to be with someone who wants the same things as you. I just don't know if that's me. You need to figure that out."

I turned to walk out, half expecting him to follow me, to beg me not to go. But he didn't. He stayed where he was, silent as I closed the door behind me.

I wasn't angry, not anymore. I wasn't even upset. I felt hollowed out, emptied of everything I'd ever felt. No love, no hate. Nothing. Nothing but the bleak darkness of a future without Cross. One day in the future, I would be absolutely certain that I was making the right decision. But now? Right now, I could only put one foot in front of the other and try not to think about what I'd just done.

Chapter 24

Cross

This couldn't be happening. I apologized for what I'd said. We'd rectified things when it came to Tucker. I'd told Hanna about Taliyah. Things should've been fixed between us. I should've been taking her to the playroom or to my bedroom for a night of sweaty, hot sex.

Instead, I was watching her walk out of my house...and possibly out of my life. I wanted to tell her to stop, to tell her that I didn't need time.

But I did.

When I was in college, I wasn't interested in settling down even though I'd been in relationships, but that wasn't abnormal for a man in his early twenties. Then I'd taken over the family business after my parents' deaths and my life became all about preserving their legacy. I hadn't given a single thought to anything besides the business. I certainly hadn't been looking for a girlfriend.

Then I met Hanna.

And I hadn't wanted anyone else from the moment I laid eyes on her. That hadn't changed. I didn't want another woman sharing my bed, sharing my life.

183

My bed. *My* life.

And that was the whole problem in a nutshell. *My*. Not *our*.

Part of me wanted to be angry at her for giving me what I saw as an ultimatum. She didn't understand what it was like to be in my position, to have been self-reliant and independent for eight years. No family. No one that I needed to share with, no one to make *my* into *our*. She'd never really been on her own. She'd gone from her family to a nearby college, and then to living with her sister.

Logically, however, I knew that wasn't fair. She hadn't given me a schedule of when she expected me to get on board her family plan. She hadn't demanded that I ask her to move in with me. She hadn't even acted like it was unreasonable for me not to want a family, or to want to keep things the same.

It just wasn't what she wanted.

She apologized for assuming that we wanted the same things, but I was guilty of it too. I hadn't considered that she might have aspirations for her life beyond what we had now. It wasn't that I thought I should be the only thing she wanted – needed – but rather that we had the same goals.

So I let her walk away because I knew nothing I could say would stop her. Nothing honest anyway. I could've lied, but I loved her too much for that.

I sank down on the couch, my stomach knotting. That's where it got complicated. I loved her. I wanted her. Only her. But I couldn't promise her a future because I'd never thought about marriage, about children. Not until that pregnancy scare.

It wasn't late, but I got up and headed for my room anyway. I wouldn't be able to sleep, I knew that, but I needed to think about so many things. About the real truth behind how I'd been behaving these last couple weeks, about why I'd been avoiding discussing our problems with Hanna. The reasons why I didn't want to look into the future for anything except work.

I would examine myself, my motives as well as what I wanted, and if I couldn't give Hanna what she wanted, what she needed, I would let her go. The thought of losing her killed me, but I loved her too much to do anything else. She deserved to be happy, even if it wasn't with me.

It was the thought of her with someone else, smiling at another man, marrying him, having his child, that did it.

I barely made it to the bathroom in time. As I bent over the toilet, I knew it was going to be a long and awful night.

By dawn, I was still sick to my stomach and completely exhausted. Neither situation was one that would be likely remedied anytime soon, especially since I still had absolutely no clue what to do. I was torn between what I knew I wanted – Hanna – and what I always thought I didn't want – commitment beyond what I was willing to offer. Then there were the two things that I feared, both at such complete odds that I didn't know how I could possibly deal with them both.

I was terrified of the prospect of a future without Hanna. Waking up alone and knowing that I might never wake up next to her again. Never hold her while we watched television together. I couldn't imagine a world where the scent of her would disappear from the pillows, the sheets, that we slept on. A world where holidays went back to the way they had been for years, me working from home, or maybe polishing off some expensive scotch.

But on the other side, I was scared of what it might mean if I did let myself picture a future with her. A marriage that would end when she realized how much better she could do than me, or when I did something as stupid as I had these past couple weeks. A child who would grow to hate me because I wasn't the parent I should be.

A family I could lose in one fell swoop.

Again.

That, I believed, was something Hanna didn't understand, that she might not be able to understand. When she looked at the future, she saw the wonderful possibilities that it held. Marriage. Children. A life together.

When I looked to the future, it was filled with all of the negative things that could – or most likely would – happen. Divorce. Infidelity. Death. Pain.

And I didn't fear it only for myself. I didn't want to leave an orphan or a widow.

I didn't know why any of this had come as a surprise to me. I'd explained to Hanna the difference between lovers and sexual partners, but I'd put her clearly in the former category, and I'd never given her any reason to think that it meant anything other than a relationship that would move forward to a logical conclusion.

I needed to talk with someone, go over what I was thinking, feeling. I needed a sounding board. Feedback.

Except the person I'd turned to for that over the last several months was Hanna, and I couldn't talk to her until I'd come to a decision.

While Juliette and I had become friends, this wasn't a conversation I could have with her. Aside from the fact that it'd be awkward, she'd probably cut off my balls as soon as she saw me, especially when she found out how the conversation between her sister and I had gone.

I liked my balls where they were, so talking to Juliette was out.

I forced myself out of bed, but not because I had anywhere to go. I just didn't want to piss on my bed, so getting up was a necessity. After I was done, I splashed some water on my face and headed back into the bedroom, unsure what to do next. It wasn't until I reached for my phone to see what time it was that I realized I did have someone I could talk to.

It made sense that she hadn't come to mind sooner since I'd only known about her a short while. I didn't know Taliyah well, and I wasn't entirely sure that she was being one hundred percent truthful, but I'd found her easy to talk to over the past couple days. And she was a woman, so she might have some idea how I could fix things, what I should do.

After I cleaned up and dressed, I called her, but she didn't answer. I left a message letting her know that I planned on stopping by and that I hoped we could go to breakfast together. A nice meal, some coffee, and maybe even an answer to my problem.

She'd told me where she was staying, and Mars had confirmed it, so I drove myself over. Even for December, the day was chilly and dreary. It was past sunrise, but there wasn't much sun coming from behind the clouds. Even as I made my way through the streets, it started to rain. Nothing heavy, but the way the horizon looked told me that it would most likely continue through the day.

Great. It matched my mood.

The desk clerk looked surprised when I walked past but didn't try to stop me. In the past, I'd frequently used hotels for my trysts, including this one, but it'd been a while since I was here. The desk clerk seemed to remember me, though I didn't know if that was because of how often I'd come here before or because he just knew who I was. Either one was possible, but neither one mattered.

I went up to the third floor and paused outside the elevator to try to remember the room number she'd given me. I'd taken two steps to the left when I saw a door down the hall open. I froze when I recognized the man who stepped out into the corridor.

Tucker Flannagan.

I gritted my teeth. What were the chances the little bastard was staying in the same hotel as my sister? Unless...fuck me.

Was it possible that he'd been spying on me and Hanna? That he'd found out about me seeing her and had followed her here. Did he intend to try to blackmail me? Or maybe sell me out to Hanna, to make himself look more appealing by telling her that I was cheating on her?

I was going to beat the shit out of him.

I took another step, then froze as Taliyah followed Tucker into the hallway. I swore under my breath. I couldn't risk Taliyah's safety. I didn't know if Tucker could be violent, but no way in hell would I take that chance with my sister.

And then I saw her lean forward and kiss him.

Confusion exploded over me. Had he seduced her to get to me? How had he found her, figured out who she was?

"How much longer, do you think?" Tucker asked as he pulled his mouth away from hers. "I don't mind flirting with Hanna to piss off your brother, but I'd rather be flirting with you."

"I hope all you're doing with her is flirting." Taliyah's eyes narrowed. "Because if you've fucked her—"

"Hey, you know you're the only one I want," he cut her off. "Besides, I've had her, and trust me, she's not worth going back to."

I really was going to kill him.

"How much longer until you get what we need from that brother of yours so we can get the hell out of here?"

Taliyah shook her head. "A while longer. He trusts me, but I still need some time to get him to make an offer. Don't worry though. He's so spun out over that girl, he won't be thinking straight for a while. I'm sure it'll be soon."

Trembling with rage, I stepped back into the shadows before I could see or hear anything more. Or do something I'd regret later.

190

Chapter 25

Hanna

When I got back to the apartment last night, I hadn't woken Juliette. I didn't want to talk to her about what happened between Cross and me. Not last night, and not this morning. I could tell that she knew something was wrong, but she didn't ask. She'd be there if I ever decided I wanted to share.

As we went through our usual weekend routine of laundry and cleaning, the only sound in the apartment was the music Juliette had turned on during breakfast. While I felt far from being at peace, there was something soothing about the mindlessness of the tasks I was doing.

By the time we sat down to lunch, I felt more open to having a conversation, though I still wasn't at the point where I wanted to talk about Cross.

"Did Dalton say anything about how he thought things went on Friday?" I broke the quiet first.

Juliette raised an eyebrow that told me she didn't believe for a moment that I wasn't deflecting...but she answered my question, "He liked you both."

"He seems like a good guy," I said truthfully and

191

studied her for a moment. "Did the two of you talk?"

She raised an eyebrow as a flash of lightning shone through the window.

"Come on, Juliette. You know what I'm talking about." I glared at her without any malice. "You can't really dance around the subject for long. Sort of on a time table."

She leaned back and ran her hand over her stomach. It was still flat, but I knew it wouldn't remain so for long. If she terminated the pregnancy, she'd want to do it before she started to show. If not, she was enough like me that she'd want to make sure that she had answers in place by the time anyone started to ask questions.

"We talked," she admitted.

Finally, something that might distract me from the gnawing in my stomach that hadn't yet faded. "And?"

"I'm keeping the baby."

Relief went through me. I would've supported her no matter what, but I was glad it'd be support given to a niece or nephew as well as a sister.

"And Dalton?" I hadn't been lying when I said I liked him. He and Juliette might not have known each other well, but I had a feeling that the two of them were a good fit.

"He wants to be involved," she said. "And not just off and on. I told him I didn't want that. If he was going to be part of our child's life, he had to decide if he wanted to be a birth certificate and birthdays kind of dad, or involved completely. Doctor visits. Being there when the baby's born. Co-parenting."

"And he's going to do all that?"

I couldn't stop the pang of jealousy that went through me. Juliette and Dalton had met once. Had no other connection except one night of sex. Cross and I had been together for months, had a relationship based on more than sex.

And yet it was Dalton who stepped up and accepted the responsibility of having a child he hadn't planned on. Dalton, who'd barely had the time to adjust to the idea of being a father but had made the choice to do what he knew was right for his son or daughter.

"And the two of you?" I asked.

She shrugged, looking away as her cheeks turned pink. "We haven't made any decisions about that."

I folded my arms and leaned back in my chair. "And why not?"

She rolled her eyes. "Because neither one of us wants to jump into a relationship just because I'm pregnant."

"But you won't completely write it off, right? Because that would be stupid." I managed a smile that didn't feel completely fake. "He's gorgeous, you know."

"I'm not blind."

"I was starting to wonder."

She threw a napkin across the table at me. "We're not saying it won't happen, okay? We'll spend time together, get to know each other. Even if nothing romantic comes of it, we both agreed that we needed to know more about each other for our child's sake."

"And if something more does come of it?" I asked.

"We'll let it," she said simply. "We won't force anything one way or the other. If we happen to find that we want something more than a platonic relationship, then we'll see if it works, but we've already decided that our child comes first, before anything we might want."

I reached across the table and took her hand. "Whatever you need, I'm here."

"Thank you." Her tone grew serious. "And you know I'm here for you, right?"

A lump formed in my throat, and I nodded, not trusting myself to speak. Maybe I'd confide in her at some point, but it wasn't now. I couldn't bear to repeat what happened between Cross and me. Not yet. It was too fresh, too raw.

A pounding at the door made both of us jump. We'd tuned out the storm outside almost automatically. Natives of LA might've had a difficult time doing it, but we were from Ohio. The weather changed so often there, we could have sun one minute and a storm the next.

"I'll get it," Juliette said as she stood.

I got to my feet as well, intending to clear the table. I didn't get past picking up a single dish, however, because a haggard and wet Cross rushed into the room, followed by Juliette, who looked both pleased and pissed.

I completely understood the differing emotions because I felt them too. Part of me was happy to see him, knowing that it had to be something important that drew him from his house on a stormy Sunday when he could've just called or texted. This was something that merited face-to-face communication, and the fact that he came to me rather than set up a meeting gave me hope as to what he wanted to say.

"I'll give you two some privacy," Juliette said as she left the kitchen.

We stood there a moment in awkward silence before he blurted out, "Tucker's using you to get to me."

Not even anywhere close to what I thought he would say. I was pretty sure my mouth was hanging open as I stared at him, but I couldn't form the thought necessary to close it. I could barely think at all. He'd clearly been jealous of Tucker before, but that had at least made some semblance of sense. Tucker was my ex and the only other person I'd ever slept with. I could see Cross not liking him just for that. But to claim that the only reason Tucker had come back into my life, the only reason he'd been flirting with me, was to get to Cross...it was beyond insulting.

"Are you fucking kidding me?" I found my voice, even if the words didn't come out as strong as I'd intended.

"I'm serious." He took a step toward me. "Please, listen to me."

I would, but not for the reason I was sure he wanted. I would listen to whatever shitty reason he'd come up with as to why this accusation was the best way to either win me back or justify his actions, and then I'd tell him to get the hell out of my life and that I didn't want to see him ever again.

I'd been honest, opened myself up to him, and all I'd asked in return was that he be honest with me. Instead, he'd come up with some bullshit about Tucker.

"Say what you came to say." I set my jaw and prepared to listen.

A look of relief crossed his face. "It's not just Tucker. It's Taliyah too."

I frowned. His half-sister? What did she have to do with anything?

"I went to her hotel this morning to talk things over with her–"

"What things?" I interrupted. I wasn't sure which would be worse. If he'd wanted to talk to her about us, or if he'd completely pushed us aside so he could focus on her.

His eyes slid off to the side, then back to me. "I needed someone to talk to about what was going on, and since she's my sister..." His voice trailed off for a moment, and then he shook his head. "That's not the point."

I planned on disagreeing with him on that as soon as he was done with the rest of his little speech.

"When I got there, Tucker was coming out of Taliyah's room."

I was surprised, but in reality, all that told me was that the two of them knew each other. Not exactly damning evidence, but I kept my mouth shut.

"She kissed him and then they started talking about how she was supposed to get me to give her money, and how Tucker was supposed to keep coming between us so I'd be more distracted."

My nails bit into my palms as the anger inside me rose from a simmer to a boil.

"She even said something about how she didn't want him sleeping with you, like she was calling the shots, and he said he wouldn't do that again—"

"Enough!" I snapped. "I thought you actually heard me when I told you how I felt, what I needed."

"I did," he protested.

"Clearly you didn't, because instead of talking about anything important, you're blaming all of it on Tucker and Taliyah, and acting like this is all some big conspiracy centered on you. Reality check, Cross." I took a step toward him. "Life doesn't revolve around you."

"That's not what...Hanna, please." He reached for me, and I took a step back. "I came to warn you that Tucker is trying to manipulate you. You and Juliette both. He isn't the man you think he is."

"Are you kidding me?" I laughed. "Tucker isn't the man I think he is? After everything, that's what you're going with? That I'm such a bad judge of character that you need to protect me from him?"

"That's not—"

"Maybe you should hear him out."

Juliette's voice came from behind me, and I glared at her as I turned. "You're on his side now?"

She shook her head. "No. I'm on your side, but if what Cross says is true, we need to be careful."

"I'm telling the truth." He sounded almost desperate for me to believe him, but I wasn't sure I could trust the reasons behind it.

"It doesn't matter why Tucker's here." I addressed Juliette, keeping my back to Cross. "He hasn't asked either of us for money, hasn't even asked me out on a date. All he's done is talk to us and apply for a job." I paused, and then added, "It sounds more like someone's jealous of anyone else paying attention to me."

Juliette's gaze flicked over my shoulder to where Cross stood. "Jealousy or not, if he's working with this woman to get to Cross, we need to take it seriously." Off of my look, she added, "I wasn't eavesdropping. The two of you aren't exactly quiet, you know."

My shoulders sagged as I realized that, no matter what she said, my sister wouldn't have my back in this. With Cross saying that Tucker was trying to use us, the application for a job came across as nefarious. Considering the issues Juliette had with her prior assistant, I could understand her desire for caution, but she could've done it without taking Cross's side.

"You know what," I looked from one to the other, "why don't the two of you go ahead and discuss whatever you need to discuss since you seem to have it all figured out. I have some things of my own to work out, so I'll step out for a while."

I didn't wait for a reply as I headed for the door. I slipped on a pair of sandals and hurried out, not even bothering to take an umbrella or jacket.

Which I regretted the moment I stepped outside and was soaked clean through. I gritted my teeth, wrapped my arms around my waist, and began to walk. I knew it was sheer stubborn pride that kept me from going back inside, but I clung to it anyway. At the moment, it was the only thing I had left, and I wouldn't give it up.

If I did, I was afraid I might break down completely, and I refused to give Cross – or anyone else – that satisfaction. I didn't know what my next move would be, but I did know that I was done getting yanked around. I knew what I wanted, and I wasn't about to settle for second best.

Chapter 26

Cross

I watched Hanna leave, barely able to believe that it was happening again. She was walking out on me for the second time – and from her own place, no less. I found myself as hopeless as I had been the day before, unable to find the words to get her to stay. I couldn't even tell her that the weather was too bad for her to go outside. Every word I thought became caught in my throat before I could get it out.

A sharp slap on my arm drew my attention from the door to Juliette. She glared up at me, her expression so much like her sister's that it made my heart hurt.

"What the hell, Cross?!"

"I'm not lying, Juliette," I protested. "I really did see Tucker with my half-sister, and they really were talking about how they were using Hanna–"

"I believe you," she cut me off. "But that's not the point."

"I know," I agreed. "She doesn't believe – ow!"

She'd hit my arm again, harder this time. "Not. The. Point."

I scowled. "Then you'll have to tell me what the point is, because I have no clue."

She rolled her eyes. "Yeah, you are pretty clueless."

I should've been insulted, but I didn't care about that at the moment. I needed to know what to do, and Juliette was apparently going to help me out rather than castrate me. My balls and I were grateful.

"I don't know what went down between the two of you yesterday, but I'll about guarantee that it wasn't because of Tucker or whoever that girl is."

"Taliyah," I supplied. "She claims she's my half-sister..."

Juliette raised an eyebrow.

"Right, sorry," I apologized. "Go on."

"Whatever it was, you came in here talking about something else," she said. "You completely dismissed her concerns, the things that she felt were important just so you could tell her what you thought she needed to know."

"I was looking out for her," I argued.

"You were being an ass about it," Juliette countered. "Your intentions may have been good, but you acted like what she cared about wasn't important."

Dammit. She was right.

"You're a Dom, Cross. You should know better."

Again, she was right, and it hurt. I did know better. I would've looked down on any Dom who'd treated his or her Sub the way I'd just treated Hanna.

I needed to fix this.

"What should I do?"

Another smack, but this one not quite so hard. "If you care about her even half as much as I think you do, you need to go after her. If you don't, then let her go."

"Of course I care about her!" Indignation burned through my despair. "I love her, Juliette!"

"Then you need to tell her that."

"I have." I ran my hand through my wet hair, flicking

droplets of water off my fingers.

"Well, obviously, there's something you haven't told her because she wouldn't have left otherwise. And if she really meant something to you, you wouldn't have let her go."

"Dammit, Juliette!" I spun to face her. "She's everything to me! I don't care about Taliyah or Tucker or any of that shit! Only her!"

Even as I said the words, the reality of them sunk in. She was everything. My past, present, and future. She was the only woman I ever wanted, so why had I thought that I needed time to tell me that?

I didn't bother telling Juliette where I was going, but I doubted I needed to. I ran back out into the downpour, squinting as I looked both ways, trying to see where she'd gone. For a few terrifying seconds, I thought she'd left and that I wouldn't be able to find her, but then I saw her flagging down the lone taxi.

"Hanna!" I called her name as I ran, certain that, at some moment, I'd slip and fall. "Hanna!"

She stopped even as she reached for the door handle.

"Please, don't leave!" I was panting as I skidded to a stop in front of her. I grabbed her hands and pulled her toward me. "Please don't leave me, baby."

Her eyes were wide as she looked up at me. I cupped her face and bent my head to kiss her. Her lips parted with a gasp, and I swept my tongue inside, claiming her mouth, claiming her. She stiffened for a moment but didn't pull away. I buried one hand in her hair, using the other one at the small of her back to keep her body flush against mine. The rush of having her in my arms came as much from the fact that I been terrified that it'd never happen again, as from her physical proximity.

"Cross," she whispered my name as she broke our

kiss. "It's raining."

"It is." I chuckled as I opened the taxi door. She climbed in, and I went after her. "Thanks for waiting," I said to the driver. I gave him my address, then turned my attention back to Hanna.

"You came after me." She looked at me as if she couldn't quite believe it.

"I'll always come after you," I promised. I wrapped my arms around her again and pulled her to me. The cab had the heat on, but I knew we'd both be chilled before we got home.

"What—"

"I'm an idiot." My admission stopped whatever she was about to say, and I didn't wait to let her start again. She needed to hear it all. "I shouldn't have needed to think about anything. You've been the only one for me from the first moment I met you, and I don't want anyone else. The only thing I want to see when I look in the future is you."

She stirred in my arms, tilted her head back so that she could look at me.

"I don't need time. I just need you." I brushed back the wet curls. "No matter what happens, it's only you." I gave her a partial smile. "Even if something happened and we had no money, if we could never have sex again, I'd still want to be at your side."

The way her eyes were shining, I could see that she understood exactly what I meant. She put her hand on my thigh, sending a bolt of heat through me. She leaned up and put her lips against my ear.

"I hope that doesn't mean that you don't want to fuck me."

I sucked in a breath.

"Because I definitely want to fuck you."

Her hand moved to my crotch, and I cursed the storm that kept us from being able to go faster.

Despite how turned on I was, I used the ride to my place to make sure Hanna understood that I would, one day, want marriage and family with her. I didn't want there to be any misunderstandings. Ever.

She kissed me then, and we barely came up for air even as we exited the taxi and made our way through the house, peeling off our wet clothes as we went. By the time we reached the bedroom, we were both deliciously naked, skin slick with rain as we fell onto the bed together.

I slid down her body, spreading her legs as I went. She whimpered the moment my tongue touched her, then cried out when I put my mouth on her. I felt like it'd been eons since I'd tasted her. My fingers dug into her hips, holding her as still as possible while I delved into her depths. I dipped my tongue into her, then moved up to tease her clit, reveling in the sounds she made. Knowing that I was the only man who'd ever get to hear her make those sounds made them so much sweeter. It was one thing to know it in some vague sort of way, but it was completely different to have said it, to know it with certainty.

As she came, I promised myself that I would do everything in my power to make sure she never regretted wanting a future with me. No matter what happened, she would always be my first priority.

I raised my head even as I slid two fingers inside her, loving the way her body arched, how her head fell back. On any given day, I'd swear she was the loveliest woman I'd ever seen, but when she was in the throes of passion, she was exquisite.

Not that I ever intended to let anyone see her this

way. A little arousal in the privacy of the club, but never like this. I was the only one who got to see her like this. The only one who'd ever know what it was like to feel her tight, wet heat. To know what it was like to wake up beside her.

She was mine.

Mine.

I twisted my fingers almost roughly, and she gasped. I moved up over her body, taking a nipple between my lips even as I thrust my fingers back into her. She dug her nails into my shoulders, deep enough to make me bite down on her sensitive flesh. She swore, her body jerking.

"Cross," she gasped. "Please, make me come again."

Suddenly, I raised my head and stilled my hand. "Move in with me."

Her eyes widened. "What?"

"Move in with me."

She squirmed, trying to move on my hand, but I nipped at her breast, making her stop without a word.

"Not the best time to be asking." Her voice was almost a whine, making me smile.

"I think it's the perfect time to ask," I countered. A twist of my hand pressed my knuckles against her g-spot, and she swore again. "Now, what do you say, Hanna? Move in with me."

"Let me come."

I bit the side of her breast hard enough to leave a mark. Her yelp was only half-pain. We'd both quickly learned that she liked teeth.

A lot.

"Move in with me."

She glared at me. "You're not going to let me come until I agree, are you?"

I grinned at her. "It makes sense." I brushed my

thumb over her clit, eliciting a gasp of pleasure. "And, besides, I don't want it to be my house, or my bedroom anymore. I want it to be ours."

Another twist of my fingers and she whimpered.

"Come on, baby. Move in with me."

Her body clenched as I made hard circles around her clit, and I knew she was close. With my free hand, I pinched and rolled her nipple.

"Hanna, love, move in with me."

She cried out as she came, body shuddering and shaking. I leaned over her, let her come down as I watched. Only after her eyes opened did I make it a question.

"Will you move in with me?"

She ran her hand down my cheek, down my chest, fire burning across my skin. I'd never wanted someone as much as I wanted her. When her fingers wrapped around my erection, I let out a groan. She could undo me with a single touch.

"I will."

I pulled her against me as I sat up. Her legs wrapped around my waist, and we both moaned as I pulled her down on me. I held her there for a moment, rested my forehead on hers. Our breath mingled, and I fancied I could almost feel our hearts beating together.

"I love you," I said quietly. "With everything that's in me, Hanna. I love you."

She took my mouth this time, claimed me even as her body rocked against mine. We would have time to play later, have time for me to dominate her. This wasn't about me or even her right now. It was about us. About who we were together.

Her head fell back, and I kissed my way across her jaw and down to her neck. She gasped my name when I scraped my teeth across her throat, and the tension in my stomach twisted into something hot and primal.

"I love that," I said.

"What?" Her eyes were closed, nipples hard against my chest.

"The way you say my name when we make love."

"Cross," she moaned my name again.

"Like that." I practically growled the words as I tightened my grip on her waist. I tugged on her hair, getting another one of those wonderful sounds from her.

Damn those were hot.

"Again," I demanded.

"Cross."

I closed my eyes.

"I love you."

Pleasure crashed over me, and her body tightened as she followed me over the edge. This was it. Everything I ever needed, right here. I was crazy to think I would ever need anything else.

Chapter 27

Hanna

Last night had been amazing, not only physically so, but emotionally. I'd felt a real connection between us, different than anything we'd had before. Not that we hadn't loved each other, but this was what I'd been craving. Something more. It reminded me of how I'd felt the first time I understood the true relationship between a Dom and Sub.

We'd fallen asleep in his bed – *our* bed, if he truly meant what he said when he asked me to move in – and when I woke, I found myself still in his arms. He was sleeping, his breathing slow and steady, his heart a steady thudding against my ear. The sounds coaxed me to wakefulness, and I found myself snuggling closer to him, enjoying the feel of his arms around me.

Yet even in the warmth and safety of his embrace, my mind couldn't help but start going over everything that happened. Not only the good, not the pleasure, but the promises made. As much as I wanted to believe that he hadn't said any of those in the heat of the moment, but rather because he meant them, I knew that I wouldn't fully believe it until it had stood for longer than a few hours.

I loved him, and I trusted him with my body, to know my limits. I wasn't certain, however, that I completely trusted him with my heart again. Not until I saw that things weren't going to just go back to how they were.

When he stirred, I waited for him to say something about work and how he'd call me later today. Something to make sure things were at status quo.

"When did you want to do it?" His voice was still thick with sleep as he tightened his arms around me.

Puzzled, I rolled toward him so we were facing each other. "Do what?" He never referred to sex as *it*, so I didn't think that was what he was asking.

If my brain had been working a little better, I would've also realized that if he'd wanted sex, he wouldn't have asked me a question. He would've kissed me, touched me, used his considerable talents to arouse me, until I was begging for him.

"When do you want to move in?" He clarified his statement, but it didn't make me any less confused. He smiled at me as he brushed curls back from my face. "You do remember that I asked you to move in with me, and after some prompting, you agreed."

I swallowed hard, a warm flush coming over me as I remembered exactly what sort of *prompting* Cross had done to convince me to agree. I hadn't hesitated because I didn't want to live with him. My hesitation had come from the fact that I wanted it so badly that I couldn't bear the thought that his offer hadn't been genuine.

"I did."

Cross's expression sobered, the look in his eyes telling me that he had an idea of what I was thinking.

"I won't hold you to anything you don't truly want," he said. "You know that, right?"

I knew if I wanted him to be honest with me, if I wanted the new, tenuous chapter of our relationship to last, I had to continue to show honesty myself.

"I want it," I said. "But only if it's what you really want. I don't want to pressure you into anything either. I never wanted that."

He sat up so quickly that it startled me. His hands came to my face, cupping my cheeks between them. "Listen to me, Hanna, my love. You didn't pressure me. You didn't make me do anything that I didn't want to do. Didn't make me say anything I didn't want to say. I meant every word, including asking you to move in with me."

The hope inside me was almost painful, and when he bent down to brush his lips across mine, it burst, flooding me.

"You are my future, Hanna." His fingers ran down my shoulders, danced across my collarbone. "And I'd be a fool to wait for it any longer."

I studied him, eyes narrowing. He was different. I wasn't sure how, exactly, or what specifically made me think that something had changed. He seemed more relaxed, more at ease with himself.

"You're sure?" I asked.

His answer came quickly, his words firm. "More sure than I've ever been."

I wanted to throw myself in his arms, tell him that I'd get my things from Juliette's today, but I held back. I wanted to make sure we did this right, and nothing would be right until we dealt with certain...issues.

"Then we'll discuss details later." When he frowned, I reached up and kissed him. "First, we have some things to talk about."

"Things?" He raised an eyebrow.

"Tucker and Taliyah."

He sighed. "Right. Tucker and Taliyah." He ran his eyes down my body and back up again. "I suppose that means we should get dressed."

A quarter of an hour later, the two of us were seated at the table, a box of gourmet bagels between us. I almost laughed at that. Back in Ohio, I never would've thought about bagels as being something that could be gourmet, but I couldn't get enough of them. The coffee in our mugs was gourmet too. Pretty much everything in the kitchen was.

"You're going to be late," I said as I glanced at the clock.

"I'm the CEO," he reminded me with a grin.

"But you like to set a good example," I reminded him this time.

"True." His smile widened. "But sometimes that means taking some time out to do what needs to be done in my personal life."

"You just have to win every argument, don't you?" I asked with a sigh.

The way his eyes danced made me want to kiss him and slap him at the same time. It was infuriating. *He* was infuriating.

But he was *mine*.

"So you're going to take the day off?"

He shook his head. "*We* are. The two of us will figure out what to do, and then we'll do it together." He reached over and took my hand. "Everything from here on out is will be together."

"I hope not everything," I teased. "I do like some surprises."

He chuckled as he released my hand and reached for his coffee. "I'll keep that in mind." After a long swallow, he continued, "But first–"

"Tucker and Taliyah," I finished.

He nodded. "What do you think we should do?"

Even though I knew he respected my opinion, I was surprised by the question. I also had absolutely no idea.

"Do they know you saw them?" I asked. I was pretty sure I knew the answer, but it was somewhere to start.

"No," he said. "They have no idea that I know what they're up to."

"And what, exactly, is that?" I asked. "You said they were talking about using me as a distraction to get money from you. Did they say how she planned to ask you for it? What she was going to say she needed it for?"

"Does it matter?" he asked. "I'm obviously won't do it."

"True," I agreed. "So do you just tell her to leave? You're pretty well-known. She may very well go public about who she is. She could tell the world that she came to you as your sister, and you turned her away. It won't look good for you."

He growled low in his throat. "I don't care how it looks."

"But we should," I countered. "I don't want her to hurt you. I don't want Tucker to hurt you."

"That little bastard can only hurt me if he hurts you." Cross's eyes flashed. "And I'll beat the shit out of him if he tries."

An idea popped into my head. "Then let's take them out at the knees."

"How do we do that?"

211

The restaurant wasn't quite as fancy as some of the ones Cross and I had gone to, but it had a pair of private rooms in the back, which was what Cross and I wanted. A pair of rooms with the ability to have the wall separating them to be withdrawn with the press of a button.

I sat in one, while Cross waited in the other. We'd made our calls back at his – *our* – place, and set up our meetings for the same early lunch. Tucker had accepted my invitation within minutes, and Taliyah had accepted Cross's as well. Now all we had to do was wait until they arrived.

"Hanna." Tucker was all smiles as he came into the room. "I'm hoping this is a celebratory lunch."

I stayed where I was, not trusting myself to meet him. Punching him in his mouth wasn't part of the plan, even though I was starting to wish it was.

"I'm really looking forward to working with you."

He was now just a couple feet from me, and I stuck my hands in my pockets to make it clear that I didn't want a hug.

"That's too bad, Tucker."

His smile froze, and I saw uncertainty flicker across his face. Good.

"You know, even after we broke up, I didn't harbor any bad feelings toward you. If you would've come to Juliette and me honestly, we would've helped you."

"I'm not sure what you mean." There was no smile now.

"You do, Tucker. You know exactly what I mean." It was my turn to smile. "I know that you've been talking to Taliyah."

His eye twitched. "I don't know–"

"Cut the bullshit." My voice was cold, flat. "What

212

are the two of you up to?"

I'd always known that Tucker was a wimp, but the moment he cracked was the first time I'd ever felt disgust for him. He spilled it all. How he'd seen an article about me and Cross, started looking for all he could find about us both. How a chance encounter in some forum had led him to someone claiming to be Cross's sister. How she'd manipulated him, convinced him that her brother owed her for the life she'd never had. How she'd used him.

It was all her fault, all her plan.

When he was finally finished, I nodded, then walked over to the switch on the wall. Without a word, I watched the wall between the two rooms pull back, revealing Cross and a pissed-off looking woman with dark blonde hair.

"All done?" I asked as Taliyah and Tucker stared at each other.

"I think so," Cross said. "You?"

"He wouldn't shut up." I grinned at him. "Told me all about how this was her idea."

"You fucking prick!" Taliyah snarled. "You're the one who wanted to throw your ex into the mix! I was fine with just going after the money."

"Come off it!" Tucker yelled back. "You loved the idea of fucking with his head! Said he deserved it!"

"While I'm enjoying the two of you fighting," Cross raised his voice, "Hanna and I really don't have the time for it."

Two sets of eyes turned to glare at us.

"I'll go to the press," Taliyah threatened. "I'll ruin you."

"I figured you'd say that," I countered. "In fact, I was counting on it."

Cross and I pulled our phones from our pockets.

213

"We have both of your confessions recorded," I said. "If either of you decide to make trouble for us, we'll release it all."

"We didn't do anything illegal," Taliyah said, her face twisted into a scowl.

"Maybe not," Cross said, lifting a shoulder. "But it sure as hell won't look good for you."

"Hanna." Tucker turned toward me. "You know—"

"Go back home," I said and dug the knife deeper, "and pray I don't let your friends or family know what you did."

The color leeched from his face. Taliyah might not have had much by the way of family, but Tucker did. Family and friends in a town small enough that it'd be bad if word got around.

Cross looked at Taliyah and I was surprised to see the flash of hurt appear on his face. "Want to know something ironic?" he said to her. "After the initial surprise, I was happy to learn you were my sister and had been thinking of how best to compensate you for the years you didn't have with my father. With me."

Taliyah's face didn't soften, she simply lifted her chin. Her expression hard as stone.

"I was thinking of the vacations we could have together. The home I would buy you. Holidays. Special occasions." His voice broke and he coughed to clear his throat. "Things we will never have now."

"Cross…" Taliyah took a step toward him, but he held up his hand, his face morphing from sad to furious.

"Get out of here." Cross's voice rang with the kind of authority that made men and women listen.

Taliyah and Tucker were no different. They hurried out the door, and Cross turned to me.

"Now," he said with a smile, "how about we get

214

some lunch and start talking about how you're going to tell Juliette that you're moving out."

Chapter 28

Cross

Christmas Eve. My second holiday with the woman I loved, and it wouldn't be the last. I just hoped it would have better memories than Thanksgiving did.

If things went my way, it definitely would.

It'd been a little over a week since Hanna and I had sent Tucker and Taliyah packing, and things hadn't gone back to normal. And I was grateful for it. I thought that I liked the routine, the knowledge that things were the same as they'd always been. But after a week of gradually bringing Hanna's things over, of turning it from *my* place into *our* place, I realized how much I would've missed if I'd insisted on never changing.

A strange sense of satisfaction went through me as I walked through the house. Hanna's clothes hung in our closet or were folded neatly in our dresser. Her pictures were now on the walls, on the mantel above the fireplace. The toiletries in the bathroom were no longer extras she brought over. She hadn't brought much, since most of the things at the apartment had been Juliette's, but it was enough to make a difference.

217

Another thing to get used to, I thought as I stepped into the living room. Hanna hadn't only been busy this week moving from the apartment to the house. She'd been appalled when I told her that I hadn't decorated for Christmas in years. I hadn't seen the point of doing it just for myself.

The entire house smelled like pine because she hadn't been satisfied with a fake tree. No, she'd managed to find a tree farm outside the city, and we'd gone out and picked a tree that was cut down right there. Last night, we decorated it, and I had to admit that it completed the look. I almost felt bad that we wouldn't be able to enjoy it longer.

Next year, I reminded myself. Anything that the two of us hadn't gotten to do this year, we'd do next year. We'd make our own traditions and memories. We had all the time in the world to do it. This Christmas, we were staying in California and had already made plans with Juliette for tomorrow. Tonight, however, was all about Hanna and me.

While things had been good between us, they'd also been busy. Now that things were resolved, we were both looking forward to a quiet evening at home with just the two of us. No more sibling / ex drama.

I'd gotten my closure about Taliyah two days ago. My PI, Mars, had gotten back to me with an apology that it'd taken him so long. Some residents of Nashville hadn't been that receptive to his bribery attempts, so he'd been forced to rely on a few technical tricks to find the information I'd wanted.

Taliyah was my half-sister. She hadn't lied about that. Aside from a birth certificate with our father's name on it, Mars had found a paternity test...along with an unsent letter. While there was always a possibility that

Taliyah's mother had contacted my father some other way or at some other time, the evidence Mars had found suggested that my father had never known about her.

And contrary to what Taliyah told me, she hadn't known who her father was until recently. Her mother had passed away from cancer like Taliyah had said, but it wasn't until then that she'd found her birth certificate and the paternity test. Mars had spoken with a friend of hers who'd filled in enough of the blanks to confirm that Taliyah had never known who her father was prior to her mother's death.

So while I was going into the new year knowing that my parents hadn't been faithful to each other, I wasn't burdened with thinking that my father had abandoned his child. I didn't know what arrangement my parents had regarding their sex lives, and from my own experiences, I knew that every relationship was different. I could accept that things might not have been as traditional as I always thought. That had been their business. However, I had been struggling with the idea that my father could've walked away from a child. Now, I knew that wasn't the case, and a weight felt like it'd been lifted from my shoulders.

The front door opened, interrupting my thoughts.

"Next time you forget something on Christmas Eve, you can go out and..."

Hanna's voice trailed off as she came into the living room and stopped. Her eyes widened when she saw what I'd done while she was gone.

Strawberries and oranges. A myriad of chocolate, both melted and solid accompanied more kinds of nuts than I'd known existed. Expensive cheeses and equally expensive crackers. The entire table in front of the couch was covered. Next to the table was a bottle of her favorite champagne.

Her eyes narrowed. "You didn't forget to buy wine for tomorrow, did you?"

I smiled at her, anticipation and anxiety twisted together in my stomach until I knew I wouldn't be able to eat.

"This is amazing, Cross." She wrapped her arms around my neck and gave me a firm kiss. It was mostly innocent but held the promise of less innocent things to come.

She went to the kitchen to drop off the wine we hadn't needed, and I poured us both glasses of champagne, then took a breath to try to steady my nerves.

It didn't work.

"Everything looks wonderful," she said as she came back into the room. She stopped in front of me and frowned. "Are you okay?"

I nodded and held out a hand. She took it and I led her over to the couch where we sat down. I handed her a glass and we each took a drink. I could see the confusion on her face when I set my glass down and took hers to do the same thing. I took both of her hands, warmth flowing through me as she wrapped her fingers around mine.

"You know that when I first approached you, I didn't know who you were," I began, "but I think – I *know* – that some part of me recognized who you were. While I've always believed that some people find love, I've never been the sort of man who believed in soulmates. Until I met you. I could see your strength, but I still wanted to protect you, take care of you."

She squeezed my hand, but I could tell she still didn't understand where I was headed.

"In my life, I've divided the women who shared my bed into lovers or sexual partners, and from moment one, you were the former. What I haven't allowed myself to admit until recently is that there's a third category, one that goes beyond anything I've had before."

I released one of her hands and reached over to retrieve the small box that I had hidden behind a plate of strawberries. Her grip suddenly tightened, and I heard the sharp intake of breath as she realized what I was doing.

"I don't just want a sexual partner or even a lover." I turned back to her and met her gaze. "I want a wife."

I opened the box, but she didn't take her eyes off me.

"There's no point in sitting around and waiting for what I know is inevitable. We belong together, Hanna, and I want everyone to know it. A few months ago, you accepted my collar, knowing that it would tell everyone in our world that you were mine. Now, I'm asking for you to accept this ring so that everyone we meet, everyone who sees you, will know that I belong to you."

"Oh, Cross." Her voice trembled, and her eyes sparkled with unshed tears.

"Will you marry me?"

A tear made a trail down her cheek as she nodded. Her hand was shaking as I slipped the ring onto her finger. I had it custom made so that it matched her collar, but she wasn't looking at it. She was looking at me. As soon as the ring was in place, she kissed me, and I could feel everything she was feeling. Desire. Joy. Love. All of it came through the bruising force of her lips on mine.

I wrapped my arms around her as I took control of the kiss. One hand slipped under the back of her shirt, my palm skimming up her spine. The other hand moved over her hip and down her thigh until I reached the bottom of her skirt. Her fingers curled into my hair as she arched against me, her desperation fueling my own. If I didn't pull back now, I would take her like this, skirt up around her hips, panties pulled to the side. While the thought of something hard and fast appealed to me, I had plans for how this was going to go.

"Slow down," I whispered against her lips. "I'll get you there, I promise, but I want to make this last."

She made a noise of protest as I moved back, but didn't argue. I took a moment to appreciate the sight of her like this. Hair mussed, lips slightly swollen, pupils wide, skin flushed.

"Undress," I said as I stood. By the time I had everything but my boxer-briefs off, she was completely naked.

Damn, she was gorgeous.

"Lay down."

I'd spread a blanket over the couch, and as Hanna moved to do what I asked, she noticed it for the first time. She gave me a questioning look but didn't say anything as I sat on the edge of the couch.

I reached over and picked up a strawberry. "White, milk, or dark?" Off of her confused expression, I clarified, "What type of chocolate?"

"Dark," she breathed.

I dipped the berry into the melted dark chocolate, and Hanna opened her mouth in anticipation. I didn't go there though. Instead, I used the strawberry to spread chocolate over her nipple. She gasped and squirmed at the combination of heat and friction. Her nipple puckered, making a hard little tip that begged for me to taste it.

I resisted as I took the strawberry back to the chocolate and dipped it again. This time, I offered her a bite. My stomach tightened as she let me feed her. This was an aspect of the Dom / Sub relationship that I hadn't explored before her, another way for me to take care of her.

The last bite of fruit went into her mouth, and I swore as her tongue darted out to lick the juice from my fingertips. If I'd been a man with less self-control, I would've been inside her in two seconds.

I selected an orange slice this time and used it to spread chocolate over her other nipple before feeding her the fruit. Only after it was gone did I lower my head to her breast and set to work cleaning off the chocolate. Her nails bit into my shoulders as I licked and sucked her soft skin, removing every last trace of chocolate from her breast, then turning to the other.

By the time I finished, she was panting, and my erection was throbbing.

But I wasn't done yet.

I selected another strawberry but didn't put anything on it this time. I ran it around her nipples, then down between her breasts, over her stomach. I watched as her eyes widened and knew she'd just realized where I was going. Or, rather, where the strawberry was going.

Her body jerked when the tip of it touched her clit, and I rubbed the fruit around and over the sensitive nerve bundle until soft mewling sounds fell from between her lips. Only then did I drop lower, dragging the berry between her folds until I was sure it was coated in her arousal.

When I raised it to her lips, she didn't hesitate. Her eyes locked with mine as she ate the entire thing. As she finished, she ran her tongue over her lips, and it took everything I had not to push my cock inside. Instead, I bent my head to claim her mouth, allowing my tongue to do what I wanted my dick to do.

"On your side," I ordered as I stood again.

She rolled onto her side as I pulled off my underwear, then I moved to stretch out behind her. I pressed a kiss to the side of her neck as I ran my hand across her stomach, then up to cup one of her breasts. I could never get enough of this body, of this woman. The glittering rock on her finger reminded me that I wouldn't have to worry about that.

I reached down to grasp her thigh, pulling her leg back enough for her to open to me. With one smooth thrust, I buried myself inside her, both of us groaning at how tight she was. A shudder ran through her, then another. I hadn't hurt her, but I knew she was feeling every inch of me right now.

I curled my fingers around her hip, holding her steady. My lips brushed the shell of Hanna's ear when I spoke, "Touch yourself. Come as much as you want. But once you start, you're not allowed to stop until I finish. Understood?"

Another shudder. "Yes, Sir."

The couch didn't give us quite as much room to move as I would've liked, but it worked better for the food, and after watching her eat that last strawberry...I was already planning other ways to incorporate similar scenarios into our sex life.

When I began to move, I kept each stroke slow, drawing all the way back until only the tip of me remained inside, then pushing forward. It was the most exquisite torture, having her squeeze me tight, feeling her clenching around me, but not driving into her the way part of me wanted to.

I swore when I saw her hand moved down between her legs, felt her fingers brush against my cock as it moved in and out of her. She came almost instantly, crying out as her muscles seized. I closed my eyes and kept up my pace even as her pussy contracted around me. As I'd instructed, she didn't stop, turning one orgasm into another, each one making it harder for me not to completely lose control.

Only when her body was limp, her whimpers telling me that she'd reached her limit, that pleasure was close to turning into pain, did I let myself go. I wrapped my arms around her, held her in place as I slammed into her once, twice, then a third time. I groaned her name as I emptied inside her, my pleasure heightened by the feel of the cool metal and hard rock on her finger.

She was mine. Forever and always.

She was my future.

Chapter 29

Hanna

"Juliette! Juliette!"

My sister and I both turned toward our mother as she came into the small side room where the two of us were making last minute preparations.

"Dalton wants to know where you put the diaper bag. Anthony needs to be changed before the ceremony starts."

Juliette sighed. "It's right where I left it, Mom, and you know it. You saw me set it out of the way."

Her voice was even, but I could see the frustration on her face. Not frustration with Dalton, who was absolutely wonderful with their son, but rather with our mother. While things between our parents and I had gotten better, they hadn't gone so well with Juliette. As we'd predicted, they'd been scandalized when she'd told them she was pregnant, even more so when they learned she wasn't at least engaged to the father. Even now that she and Dalton were officially dating, our parents weren't happy.

Case in point, from the moment our parents had arrived in California, they'd been...*overly helpful* when it came to offering parenting advice. It didn't matter that Juliette and Dalton had been doing a fine job these past three months. Everything was about all the things RJ and Abbie were doing right with their little Susan, all the ways Juliette and Dalton weren't doing with Anthony.

"Mom," I cut in. "Could you go get the bag and give it to Dalton? I need Juliette to help me finish doing up the back of my dress."

"I can help you," Mom offered. "Juliette should take care of her son."

"Juliette is standing right here," my sister muttered. She kept her voice low though. She promised me that she'd hold her tongue today.

I hadn't made any such promises.

"Well, I can assure you that his father is quite capable of taking care of him." I gave Mom a wide smile. "And if you don't feel like you can find the bag and take it to Dalton, I'd be more than happy to do it for you."

The expression on Mom's face turned brittle. "No, dear. It's your wedding day. I'll go."

Juliette waited until the door closed before she laughed. "I hope you don't talk to Cross like that."

I grinned at her. "Not unless I'm in the mood to get spanked." I fell silent for a moment, my levity fading. "Can I ask you something?"

"Of course." She finished the last two buttons, and I turned toward her.

"You and Dalton started dating before Anthony was born," I began. "Was it...weird?"

"Was what weird?" Her expression suggested she had an idea of what I was asking but that she wanted to be sure.

I glanced back at the door, not because I was embarrassed by the subject matter, but rather because I didn't want to even think about what our mother would say if she walked in on this particular conversation.

"Sex. Did you being pregnant make sex weird between the two of you?"

"Like physically?" She turned toward the mirror and fixed a few loose strands of hair. "Not exactly. I mean, not every position is comfortable, and afterwards, intercourse is off the table for a while."

"I figured that," I said. "I meant more with the whole, you know, Dom / Sub thing. Was it strange, doing all that when you were pregnant? Or did you guys stick with vanilla sex?" I could feel the heat rising in my face. "I don't want to ask Cross because I don't want him to think I'm worried–"

"It varies from person to person," she said, turning to face me now. "And it'll be different for the two of you since you're his submissive unlike Dalton and me. But, how far you want to go, you'll want to discuss with him."

There was another moment of silence before I asked the question that had really been nagging at me on and off for the past couple days. "So it doesn't feel strange to be a parent and..."

She chuckled. "You mean the fact that Dalton and I could be in the middle of a scene where I'm flogging him, and then have to take a break to change Anthony's diaper?"

I laughed, the tension in me easing. "Exactly."

She shrugged. "It's who I am. Both a dominant and a mother. I don't feel the need to define myself as only one or the other."

I nodded, absorbing what she said. Of the four of us, Dalton may have been the newest one to the group, but I was still the newest to the lifestyle. I wasn't ashamed of what we did or who we were, but there were still times I struggled to balance it with the rest of my life.

A knock at the door, and then Abbie stuck her head

in. "It's time."

"Thank you."

Abbie flashed a smile at me and then disappeared.

"You ready?" Juliette asked.

I looked at myself in the mirror, took in my reflection. My dress was simple enough, an off-white with very little busywork. It hugged my curves, showed off a modest amount of cleavage. Instead of a veil or some fancy crown, I'd had baby's breath arranged in my curls. The only jewelry I wore, aside from my ring, was my collar. No one attending the wedding, aside from three others, would know its true nature, but Cross would know why I wore it, and that was all that mattered.

"I think I was ready to marry him the day I woke up in his house, and he told me he was going to take care of me."

I'd wanted a fall wedding, and wanted to give Juliette enough time to recover after Anthony's birth, so we'd set it for October. The weather was perfect. Not too hot, not to cold. The church had been my concession to my parents, who hadn't been happy that Cross and I had decided on only having Dalton and Juliette as our attendants. In their minds, RJ was the natural choice for best man, which of course meant that Abbie needed to be paired with him as my maid of honor.

Things could've gotten bad if Abbie hadn't shocked us all by speaking up. In a calm, matter-of-fact manner, she told my parents that she supported my choices because it was my wedding, not theirs. Then, to top it all off, she told RJ to stop being a selfish ass and stick up for his sisters.

I was pretty sure if it hadn't been for the fact that she'd just given birth less than forty-eight hours before, there might've been further disagreement, but no one in my family was crazy enough to argue with a woman who'd gone through twenty-two hours of labor.

After that, things had gotten a bit easier for me. It also helped that my parents had fallen in love with Cross the moment he put that ring on my finger. He talked business with my dad, charmed my mother, and often played mediator between us. We'd never be close, but I was at least able to have a wedding without drama.

An absolutely beautiful wedding and an even more beautiful reception. We'd decided to have at an outdoor venue that allowed for an indoor option if the weather was bad. It wasn't, so now I was dancing with my husband in a clearing surrounded by flowers. The scent was heady, a perfect combination of all the right plants. I didn't know how the wedding planner Cross had hired had found it, but I made a note to myself to give her a bonus when we got back from our honeymoon.

"What are you thinking about, Mrs. Phillips?" Cross asked as he spun me around.

I laughed. Mrs. Phillips. "Just thinking your wedding planner needs a bonus."

He frowned.

"What's wrong?" I immediately looked around, trying to figure out what had caused the shift.

"Here I am, thinking you're counting down the minutes until you can ravish me, and you're thinking about our wedding planner."

I leaned closer and put my mouth against his ear. "Maybe you should think about ways to punish me then?"

The hand on the small of my back flexed, the only physical indication I received that Cross had heard me.

"A toast!" RJ called.

Shit.

When Cross started to pull back, I tightened my grip around him. I'd hoped to do this on our honeymoon, but Cross was bound to notice if I asked for something other than champagne for the toast.

"Are you okay?" he asked, concern on his face.

I nodded, then smiled, though there was a bit of nervousness to the smile. "Before we do that, I should mention something. I ordered sparkling grape juice for tonight."

"Okay?" He sounded as confused as he looked.

"Because I can't have champagne."

I waited, watched his eyes widen. He'd never given me any reason to doubt any promises he'd made, but this was different. This was a strange near-repeat of what happened almost exactly a year ago.

Except with one critical difference. This time, it really was me who was pregnant.

"Hanna?" Cross stopped dancing and reached up to put his hand on my cheek. "I don't want to make an assumption here."

"I'm pregnant."

The words had barely left my mouth before he was kissing me. A deep, full kiss that I felt all the way to my toes. There was no hesitation, no doubt. I could feel the love, the acceptance. Words, I might doubt, but this...this I knew was the truth.

"I love you," he murmured against my lips. "So much."

I would've told him that I loved him too, but I was too busy trying to regain my breath.

"And I'm going to love starting a family with you."

"Come on, you two!" Juliette called out. "Plenty of time for that on the honeymoon!"

"She's right, you know. We do have the whole honeymoon for all of that."

"True." He turned us toward the others, wrapping his arm around my waist. "But I think we'll have to put in some extra time in the bedroom and the playroom over the next couple months. Once the little ones start coming, the opportunities for alone time goes down exponentially."

"Little *ones*?" I looked up at him in surprise. "As in plural?"

He kissed my temple. "What can I say? We're going to make beautiful babies."

Chapter 30

Hanna

I was putting forth maximum effort to smile and be supportive as my sister asked me for the thousandth time if her hair looked good. I didn't blame her for it. It was her wedding, after all. And I was excited for her. I loved Dalton. He was great for Juliette and a wonderful father to Anthony. I had no doubt that they'd be as happy together as Cross and I were.

But today's temperature was a record high, and I was a week overdue. Little Bethany Mae Phillips was procrastinating so much that I had an appointment tomorrow to have labor induced. The doctor had wanted to set it for yesterday, but I told him that only an act of God would make me miss my sister's wedding.

I didn't regret it. Not really.

But I was completely miserable, and it was getting harder not to show it. Both Juliette and Dalton had offered to postpone things, but I'd refused. Our family had flown out for the ceremony, and I knew it would be almost impossible for them to stay any longer than the weekend. Well, Mom was staying through the next week, she said it was to watch Anthony while his parents went on a short honeymoon, but we all knew that a good part of it was because she was certain Cross and I would need her expertise when the baby was born.

When Dalton had proposed to Juliette on Christmas Eve this past year, our parents' attitudes toward her had softened. Neither one of us were quite to RJ's level since we hadn't moved back to Ohio, but at least we'd conformed to marital expectations at last.

The thought made me laugh under my breath. Our parents would freak out if they knew how nonconforming our relationships were, but we were fine with letting them think what they wanted.

I shifted in my seat and bit back a wince. Up until now, the pregnancy had been fairly easy. Abbie was already having a tough time with her second one, and she was only four months along. Between the two of us, at least Juliette would have a while before family started asking when she was going to have another one.

"Are you okay?" Juliette asked as she turned toward me. "There's still time to call things off."

I shook my head. "I'm fine."

The twinge in my back said that maybe I wanted to reconsider that statement, but I pushed it aside. I would get through the ceremony, and if I didn't think I could handle staying any longer, I'd excuse myself. Juliette and Dalton had asked to have the ceremony and reception here at Cross and my house since it was only immediate family, so I wouldn't have far to go to relax.

"Come on, Hanna." Mom helped me to my feet. "Let's get you to your seat."

Juliette and Dalton had opted not to have anyone standing with them during the ceremony – another thing I was grateful to them for – so my seat was next to Cross. I looked around as I settled next to him. The wedding

236

planner had outdone herself. I hardly recognized the dining room. It looked like something out of a fairy tale, all gold and lavender. The French doors let in natural light while remaining closed so we could appreciate the air-conditioning.

Juliette's assistant peeked out from the connecting kitchen door and caught my eye. She smiled and gave me a thumb's up to let me know that things were all set for the reception. She'd been a real find. Both Juliette and I felt completely comfortable leaving her in charge while we were gone over the next week, and I knew I could trust her to fill my shoes while I was on maternity leave.

Cross took my hand, threading his fingers between mine before lifting them to kiss the back of my hand. "How are you doing?"

I nodded and gave him a tight smile. Then the music changed, and Dalton was taking his place next to the minister. Another muscle spasm went through my back as I turned to watch Juliette come forward.

I finally admitted that I was lying to myself even as the minister began the ceremony. I knew what I was feeling wasn't muscle spasms. I'd been having them on and off all morning, but they'd started coming more consistently over the past hour or so. I wasn't going to ruin Juliette's wedding though. The contractions were still far enough apart that I wasn't worried. My water hadn't even broken yet. The ceremony was going to be short because of all of the young kids – Dalton had four nieces and nephews under the age of five – so I could power through it. Once everyone had gone home, then I'd have Cross take me to the hospital.

As Dalton kissed Juliette, I felt Cross watching me. It was no surprise that he was so aware of my body that he could tell something was wrong. I didn't look at him as he helped me to my feet so we could applaud, but even as I straightened, another contraction seized me, and I grabbed onto his arm.

"Hanna?" His voice was sharp enough to draw everyone's attention.

I was saved having to say it when my water broke. I looked up at him and saw concern and annoyance mingling in his eyes. He knew I'd waited. I gave him a sheepish smile that turned into a grimace as pain tightened my muscles.

His arm went around my waist, supporting me. "Juliette–"

"Go," she said. "I'll take care of things here, and we'll meet you at the hospital."

"No," I said. "You enjoy your reception."

Juliette's eyes narrowed.

"At least feed everyone so you're not eating hospital food while you're waiting."

She looked like she was about ready to argue when Dalton put his hand on her arm. "We'll all eat and get things cleaned up, then come to the hospital."

"Can someone grab my bag?"

"I'll get it." To my surprise, my brother volunteered. "Where is it?"

"Up the stairs, second door on the left, in the closet," Cross said. "It's a small black bag. Bring it out to the car."

And just like that, I went from being induced tomorrow to being rushed to the hospital to deliver naturally.

When she finally arrived, I was beyond exhausted. Every muscle in my body ached, and I felt like I was fighting to keep my eyes open. Then they handed her to me and my entire world narrowed down to the tiny, perfect human being I held in my arms. She was red and wrinkled, nothing like the newborns they always showed on tv or in the movies, but she was still the most beautiful thing I'd ever seen.

I didn't realize Cross was there until I felt him kiss the top of my head. I tore my eyes away from our daughter long enough to look up at him and see my own emotions reflected back at me.

"Thank you," he said softly.

"For what?"

"For everything. Marrying me. Giving me a daughter. A family." He reached down to touch her cheek, an expression of wonder on his face.

I'd heard it said somewhere that some men fall in love, get married, and have children, while others get married, have children, and then fall in love. I wasn't so sure about that, but at that moment, when I saw how he looked at our daughter, I fell in love with him all over again. My husband. The father of my child. The man who protected me, cared for me, watched over me.

He was mine, and I knew I'd continue falling in love with him over and over again until the day I died. Then he turned and looked at me, and I knew he felt the same.

The End

More from M.S. Parker:

The Billionaire's Mistress
Con Man
Indecent Encounter
The Client
Unlawful Attraction
Chasing Perfection
Blindfold
Club Prive
The Pleasure Series
Exotic Desires
Pure Lust
Casual Encounter
Sinful Desires
Twisted Affair
Serving HIM

Acknowledgement

First, I would like to thank all of my readers. Without you, my books would not exist. I truly appreciate each and every one of you.

A big "thanks" goes out to all the Facebook fans, street team, beta readers, and advanced reviewers. You are a HUGE part of the success of the series.

I have to thank my PA, Shannon Hunt. Without you my life would be a complete and utter mess. Also a big "thank you" goes out to my editor Lynette and my wonderful cover designer, Sinisa. You make my ideas and writing look so good.

About The Author

M. S. Parker is a USA Today Bestselling author and the author of the Erotic Romance series, Club Privè and Chasing Perfection.

Living in Las Vegas, she enjoys sitting by the pool with her laptop writing on her next spicy romance.

Growing up all she wanted to be was a dancer, actor or author. So far only the latter has come true but M. S. Parker hasn't retired her dancing shoes just yet. She is still waiting for the call for her to appear on Dancing With The Stars.

When M. S. isn't writing, she can usually be found reading– oops, scratch that! She is always writing.

Made in the USA
Middletown, DE
08 January 2021